Becoming

A Multi-Genre Anthology for Not Quite Adults

E. Latimer, Angela Shelley, Eliza Boyd,
Katherine Bogle, Taylor Hondos,
Majanka Verstraete, Janna Jennings,
Kellie Bean

ISBN-13: 978-1-988902-13-5

To all those who haven't quite figured out "adulting" yet

THE SPELL THIEF
E. LATIMER

The better the prose is, the better the spell works.

It's easy to forget, when you're cobbling together phrases, when you're trying to find a balance. Making sure you're not so sparse that the spell doesn't do what you want it to, or so flowery that it randomly sets Ms. King's thousand-dollar Prada skirt on fire in the middle of fifth period.

It's the latter mistake that Oscar and Alice are discussing as I struggle to get into the library study room without dropping my books, or the coffee cup in the crook of my arm.

"You guys are never going to let me live that down, are you?" Henry groans.

Behind me Oscar leans over my shoulder and the faint scent of Old Spice reaches me. He takes the cup of coffee.

"Unless Agatha here spills black coffee all over her white blouse right after lecturing us about keeping things organized. Then we'll talk about *that* for the next two months."

I shoot him an exasperated look as I shove the study

1

room door open. The place is still tidy this early in the morning. The wide oak table in the middle is enough to seat about ten people, so it's a perfect fit for my four person study group, seeing as we like to spread our papers out all over the place.

"I wasn't talking about organizing your personal life, *Oscar.*" I flip on the light switch, flooding the room with humming yellow light. "I meant spell work. Keeping your notes organized is important." I shove my books onto the table and accept my coffee back from Oscar, who smirks at me.

"Thanks."

Oscar reaches out to tap the book on top of the pile, my leather notebook. "Well we all know how you keep organized, Jane Austen."

"Having it all in one place is common sense," Alice says. Her binder is pink, with black sharpie graffitied all across the front. Everything about Alice is like that binder, even her prose is beautiful with a touch of grit.

"Exactly, thank you." I ignore the eyebrow Oscar raises at me. "It's convenient."

"Highly convenient," Henry agrees, sliding into the nearest seat and depositing his textbooks on the table. Papers spill out of his three ring binder onto the table, and he doesn't seem to notice. "It makes it effortlessly easy for me to lose it all at once."

"Stay on target," I snatch my leather notebook off the top of the pile, placing it carefully in front of me like I always do. "We're here to discuss what happened just now."

Oscar rolls his eyes, slumping into his seat. "Aggie you're so goddamn dramatic, it was a prank, that's all, a bunch of people got together—"

"That wasn't more than one person," I say, frowning at him. Oscar is fun—and attractive, I'll admit to that—but it drives me insane that he never takes anything seriously. "Someone was making a statement, and I don't like it."

Henry shifts in his seat, clears his throat. He flinches slightly when I look over at him.

"You've clearly got something to say."

"Yeah," he hesitates, glances over at Alice, who shrugs. "It doesn't seem like a big deal, Aggie. Do you think maybe because the competition is coming up you're feeling especially sensitive?"

"Threatened, you mean?" I fold my arms over my chest and glare around at them. "Yeah, I'm threatened by someone stealing my spells." I slam my book open and slide it across the table, and after a second, Henry leans forward, staring down at the page.

He frowns in concentration, then sits back, passing it on to Alice.

Oscar ignores the book when Alice tries to pass it to him. "So you're working on a water dragon spell too. Weird coincidence."

"Are you serious?" I throw up my arms. "My book went missing from my locker, Oscar. For a full hour!"

"And then you found it under your books. You misplaced it." Oscar sits back in his chair, and he actually has the nerve to put his feet up on the table.

I curl my fists under the tabletop, forcing myself not to swat at his shoes, to push him over. "I wrote out this water dragon spell yesterday. Yesterday my book goes missing. This morning we show up and there's a huge water dragon in the fountain and a magician's signature."

I snatch the book from Henry, who's examining the page with raised brows. "He signed it E. Williams. Who the hell is this E person?"

"And more importantly," Oscar says, "Why is his signature so lame? Who does a spell that badass and signs it with *Williams*? God, get a pen name, already. It's like putting fuzzy dice in a Rolls-Royce."

I narrow my eyes at him and he gives an exaggerated sigh and tucks his hands behind his head.

"I'm sure you're flying off the handle again. Your

spells aren't that similar."

I reach forward without a word and jab my finger at the notebook, and after another heavy sigh he scoops it up and tips his head to read it, eyes flicking back and forth across the page. I keep my gaze glued to him, pressing my lips together tightly. I can't stop remembering what happened, everyone crowded around the fountain ogling the twisting blue water dragon as it arced and glistened in the sunlight, incredibly detailed, beautiful. And undeniably *mine*.

The thing that hurts so much is that it wasn't finished, it wasn't done. And someone finished it for me, and it kills me to say that they did a good job.

I blink as Oscar actually sits up. He's still staring down at the book, and now there's a faint crease between his blond brows.

Henry's brows twitch upward, and Alice looks up from her binder. It should annoy me that it takes Oscar to get them to take it seriously, instead I jab a finger at my book and say, "See?"

Oscar frowns, slides the book across the table to Henry. Henry bends his dark head over the book, and he and Alice pour over it again.

So now they're taking it seriously.

"You know I'm right, don't you?"

Oscar drags a thumb across his lips, obviously thinking. I swear he even postures when he thinks, one hand tucked under his chin, elbow on the table. His black sweater is perfectly form-fitting, which is usually enough to distract me, but all I care about right now is that my friends see what I see. I'm not being crazy, this is a real thing that happened. Someone stole my spell book. Someone stole the spell that was supposed to win me the Spell Writing Championship, and used it in the goddamn water fountain, the covered-in-gum-and-graffiti, full-of-people's-dirty-pennies, water fountain.

I feel a muscle in my jaw twitch.

"It *does* seem like a similar spell," Oscar finally admits.

I don't let the triumph show on my face. "I know how hard that must have been for you."

He smirks. "Shut up. Anyways, what are you going to do about it? It's not like the guy was standing there signing autographs. And E-Fuzzy-Dice-Williams isn't going to be kicking around the halls telling everyone how awesome it was to steal Agatha's notebook. How are you going to find him?"

I smile at him, and even I can feel how predatory the expression is. "Student registry. I happen to know Ms. R takes extra-long lunches."

Oscar raises a brow. "Sometimes you scare me."

"As she should." Alice raises her voice as the bell goes off, scraping her papers together, stuffing them back into her binder. She slides my notebook back toward me. "And I agree with you. This spell is way too close for comfort."

"*Thank* you." I snap up the leather book and hold it close to my chest. "I'm glad you all agree, because I need one of you to stand watch for me outside the office during lunch."

There's a collective groan from my study group as we head toward the door.

It turns out that our first class—Technical Spell Writing—completely eliminates the need for my office break in.

We file into the classroom, me trailing behind Oscar, still muttering about his reluctance to be my lookout and to our seats near the middle of the circular classroom. It's only when I finally look up from my notebook that I see him.

He's standing next to Ms. King's desk, an easy smile on his face, his hands in the pockets of a very expensive looking leather jacket. His hair is dark, perfectly tousled to create the illusion of bedhead, and the way he stands, like he belongs here, no, like he owns the place, instantly puts my back up.

It reminds me of the first time I met Oscar, and instinctively I glance over at him. Sure enough, Oscar is glaring at the guy with open suspicion. Sheesh, it's like one peacock spotting another across the room.

I bite the inside of my cheek. Normally I'd be razzing Oscar about someone else being prettier than him, but I don't like the look of the guy either, and when Ms. King waves one hand at him, a wide smile on her face, and introduces him, I figure out why.

"Students, meet your new classmate, Edgar Williams. This is his first time in Seattle, so please make him feel welcome."

A murmur goes up from the classroom, and someone calls out over the noise, "Did you do the water dragon?"

Edgar shrugs, like he's being modest, but his cocky smile stretches wider. "Yeah, that was me."

Another murmur, this time a wave of approval, and even Ms. King says, "That was very impressive, Edgar."

I lean forward in my desk, fingers gripping the edges. My eyes burn holes in the side of Edgar's stupid face. I feel Oscar's hand on my arm and he hisses, just loud enough so I can hear him over the noise,

"Steady, Aggie. You can't win this years' competition if you turn this guy into a weasel or something."

I can't even say anything back, I'm too consumed by rage. Ms. King gestures at Edgar to sit, and he weaves between the desks, his trajectory taking him straight toward me, toward the empty desk a few spaces in front of mine.

His dark eyes scan the room, over my classmates, and his easy smile doesn't falter until he gets to me. His brows twitch upwards when he sees my face. I don't bother to hide my hostility, I glare harpoons at him. I picture him falling in the fountain, my water dragon drowning him in two feet of dirty penny-water.

"Hi," Edgar says, breezily, like he doesn't know why I'm glaring at him. Like he didn't steal my book and rip off

6

my spell.

"So nice to meet you," I grit out. "That was a very…interesting, spell you did this morning. It seemed somehow…familiar."

For a moment I think he's going to deny it, stare at me blankly. But then he grins. "Yeah? Maybe if you ask nice I'll give you lessons someday, sweetheart."

He *winks*.

Alice leans forward at her desk, her eyes fixed on my face. She whispers across me to Oscar. "Is that actual smoke coming out of her nostrils?"

For a moment Oscar doesn't answer, and when I look over I'm surprised to see his face is red, and he's practically drilling holes in the back of the new guy's head with his scowl. "That guy's a grade A jackass."

I don't know if Oscar's motivations are one hundred percent pure, or if he's just mad the guy has better hair than him, but I don't care. He's right.

Someone needs to take that guy down.

"You should go to a teacher." Henry pushes his books into his locker, jabbing at them as they try to spill back out. "You know, like a responsible adult. This isn't high school drama."

"He says, as he shoves his text books into his locker next to his *Baywatch* poster." Oscar leans against his own locker, still frowning down the hall, where new guy is now surrounded by a group of admirers. Mostly girls, I notice.

"Hey, don't mock the poster. It's a classic." Henry catches a zip-locked half of a peanut butter sandwich before it bites the dust, shoving it back on top of his *Quills and Incantations* book. He slams the locker shut. "Anyways, I'm serious. We should tell someone."

Oscar opens his mouth, no doubt to say something sarcastic.

"Maybe Henry is right," Alice says. She's staring down

the hallway too. "I mean, it is plagiarism, right?"

Henry looks surprised.

"It's not though," Oscar says, the scowl returning. "Comparatively the spells are similar, yes, but we have no way of proving his is a word for word copy unless he produces the spell work, which…why would he?"

"Why would he do this at all?" I say slowly, drumming my fingernails on the leather cover of my notebook. The thought keeps occurring to me. Why show off on his first day and risk it? Obviously I'm going to figure out it's my spell. Obviously I'm going to be pissed.

"Maybe he wants a fight," Henry suggests.

"Or maybe he thinks you're going to let him walk all over you like a doormat." Oscar says. "Like you'll just let him take all the glory for that spell and not say anything."

My fingers tap the cover harder. "That's ridiculous. He can't just rip off my spell and get away with it."

"Look at him," Oscar says. "He looks so smug."

He really is. Edgar is leaning against the old radiator at the back of the hall now, and the way he's moving his arms, he's clearly describing the dragon. Maybe telling people some of the lines from his…from *my* spell.

My fingernails are practically biting into the cover now. "He is so smug. He's just so…open about it."

"He needs to be stopped," Oscar says.

"You're just mad he's a snappier dresser than you. Plus he has better hair." Alice rolls her eyes, and Oscar looks offended. "Look, we could probably let this go. He's just some loser that can't do his own spells. He'll flunk out soon enough."

I whirl around, gripping the book so hard my fingertips feel numb. "Excuse me? He stole my spell."

"And called her sweetheart," Oscar says. "It was totally condescending."

"Just admit it's about the hair," Henry says.

I'm clutching my book so hard that it takes a few gentle tugs for Henry to pry it out of my hands.

He examines the fingernail prints on the front cover. "Maybe you should confront him."

"Let's do this." Oscar cracks his knuckles, and Henry shakes his head.

"Slow your roll. I said Aggie should, not you, He-Man."

"Yeah." I puff out my chest, trying to put the same swagger into my posture that Edgar has just standing there. Why should he act like he's the shit? He's a *thief*, I'm the victim here. I'm in the right. "I'm going to go give that guy a piece of my mind."

Alice tucks her binder beneath her arm. "Well okay then. This is the most exciting thing to happen since Alex McMillan vanished his left arm last semester. Let's do this."

I feel badass approaching him, with Alice and Oscar flanking my left and right and Henry just behind. I imagine us in slow motion. Like the cool kids from a movie. Even if he has a bunch of girls fawning over him, my posse is here to back me up. I'm cool and collected, about to take him down with my razor-sharp wit and vocabulary. I'm a writer, after all, I can turn out a sentence or two if I need to.

This guy is going down.

Edgar looks up as I approach, and his dark eyes meet mine. He smiles, a slow, lazy expression. His face is so full of arrogance that I know beyond any doubt that he *knows* me. He knows I'm the one he stole that spell from. And he knows that I know.

"You! You stole it!" I jab a finger at him, suddenly so furious I'm stammering.

He raises a brow at me, his expression condescending. "I'm sorry, what?"

"I—my...the book. You stole my book." I cross my arms over my chest, irritated

So much for razor-sharp wit.

"Not had much practice at introductions I see. Agatha

Lu, right? I'm Edgar Williams, *so* pleased to meet you."

I only blink at him, shocked, until it occurs to me that he must have seen my full name written on the inside flap of my book. I wrote my name in case it ever went missing. And my phone number.

Oh god, this jerk has my phone number.

He unfolds himself from the wall, uncrossing his arms and legs, taking a step closer to me. He's taller than I thought. The girls behind him stare at me with wide eyes and lean sideways to whisper to one another.

"That's a serious accusation, darlin'. You got any proof of that?"

"Are you *serious*?" Anger swells hot inside me, but before I can say anything Oscar bursts out from beside me,

"It's in her book!" He waves one hand at my book, which Henry holds open to the spell in question. "The spell you left in the fountain was exactly like that."

"Oh wow." Edgar shoves his hands in his pockets, raising his brows as he pretends to look over the page. "You did a water dragon too, very cool. Doesn't look finished though. Wouldn't someone have to be a *really* good magician to finish off someone else's high-level work?"

I can only glare at him in disbelief.

"Oh," Alice says. "Oh no, I know you did *not* just pat yourself on the back for being good at stealing people's work. Because that's basically an admission of guilt."

Edgar's gaze flicks to her and he shrugs, still smiling. "Yeah, that would be really nuts, wouldn't it? Good thing I didn't steal anything."

He stoops down to pick up a book bag from the floor and slings it over his shoulder. "So nice to meet you all." He smiles at me, pointedly. "I think Advanced Prose Magic is starting soon, so I'll see you around." He nods. "Agatha."

I'm in Advanced Prose too, but I take the next period off, not able to bear seeing Edgar sitting in class, all smug and superior. To my surprise Alice follows me into the study room.

"You're skipping Advanced? I thought you'd have to be bleeding to death before you skipped!"

Alice shuts the door behind her.

"Usually yes, but this guy is a special kind of emergency."

I look around at the others. Oscar and Henry are already both sitting at the table. They come here to study in their spare, and their books are open but neither of them are even looking at them. They both look at me expectantly.

"So, you guys all believe me that it was my spell and he stole it?" I clutch my notebook tightly, feeling something lighten in my chest. "You don't think I'm overthinking again?"

"Oh, you definitely overthink everything," Oscar says, but before I can get indignant he puts up one hand, "But, you're totally right in this case. This guy isn't even *trying* to hide it. I think he actually gets some kind of sick pleasure out of taunting you."

"Yeah." Henry rocks back in his chair, fingers laced over his stomach. He frowns. "Did you see his face? He's just so…"

"Smug?" I finish for him, and everyone nods. It kills me a little inside to say it, "He's right though. He couldn't have finished off that spell without being really good. So, we're up against it."

"We've got to prove somehow that he stole that spell," Alice says grimly. She sits down and flips open her binder. Flattens a page with one hand. Aside from beautiful prose, the other thing Alice is good at is lists, she's the most organized person in the group. I watch as she prints along the top of a fresh sheet of paper,

MASTER PLAN

and then draws a bold line underneath.

"Well, what's our plan? Step one?"

I hesitate. I'm usually with Alice on this one, I usually have things planned out meticulously. I'm an adult and I thought I had my life together. But now...

I've never had anything like this happen. I never thought anyone would steal my spell. Who plans for that? It was going to be my thesis, that spell. It was going to get me my final grade. And now it's gone. Used up like a cheap trick.

"Okay let's talk goals instead." Henry taps his pencil on the table. "Do we want to get this guy kicked out? Or failed?"

"I say we get him kicked out," Oscar leans forward, hands on the table. His eyes glitter as they fix on me. He's out for blood.

I open my mouth. Shut it again. Frown. Old me would have said no. That's not nice. It's petty and underhanded. But...he went out of his way to plagiarize me. And then basically rubbed it in my face with a bit of casual sexism on top.

Okay. Nice was several indignities before that. Nice evaporated in the face of his thievery.

"Yeah," I finally say. "Yeah, let's do this."

Step One: Go to teacher.

We pick Ms. King, because even though Henry set her skirt on fire she somehow still likes him. Normally Oscar takes shots at him about being the teacher's pet but now none of us are making fun. We crowd up behind him as he pauses at the door, letting everyone flow by us in the hallway. Classes are just letting out.

"We have fifteen minutes before Grammar and Alchemy," I say. I keep shifting from foot to foot, so nervous I can barely stand still. "So get in, show her the book and—"

A burst of noise interrupts me, a flood of people making their way down the hall behind us. When I turn I feel my heart jam itself up into my throat, the anger in my stomach flaring up again.

Edgar is in the middle of a crowd of people. It's not all girls this time, there are at least three guys practically hanging off him.

"Dude, that was awesome." Teagan, the guy who always sits behind me in Advanced Prose, is trailing behind Edgar. "I think I still have some in my hair."

"What…?" Oscar starts to say, and then he reaches out and snags the sleeve of the nearest girl going past. Connie Lee, who stops and gives him a huge grin.

"Did you see—" she pauses when she realizes it's Oscar. "Oh, you're not in it. Aggie, I didn't see you there. You should have seen what he did. It was amazing."

Connie has something in her hair, chunks of melting ice, it looks like.

My mouth falls open. "Is that—did he make it—"

"He made it snow in the classroom," Connie says, eyes shining. "Isn't that cool? Mr. Jackson said it was a really good spell."

I'm speechless, I can only gape at her, and the others stare at me, obviously confused. After a few seconds, when nobody says anything, Connie raises her brows at us and then shrugs, walking away.

"Aggie?" Henry pokes my arm tentatively, like I might explode and pepper everyone with Aggie shrapnel at any second. Which…I might. I feel like I'm about to explode.

Hands shaking, I snatch the leather book out of my bag, mumbling angrily to myself as I flip through to the last page, the one right next to the water dragon spell. "There," I jam my finger into the page. "It's right *there*."

Oscar leans over, gently taking the book from me, and he, Henry and Alice pour over the page. I shut my eyes, seeing bursts of electric light in the blackness behind my eyelids. This cannot be happening.

"Oh shit," Alice says.

"The Snowglobe," Henry reads. "She tips her head back to look at ceiling, at the tiles, at the humming electric lights. The cold gathers inside her belly, inside her chest, inside the tips of her fingers—"

"Okay, okay," Alice says, sounding alarmed. "Stop there, we get it. You're going to make it snow in the hallway too."

"So," Oscar says, looking sideways at me. "The question is, exactly how many of your spells did this guy take?"

The study room again, another emergency meeting. This time it's nearly going on six and all of us are getting hungry. Oscar wanders outside the room and into the library in search of reception, attempting to put in an order for pizza on his cell.

For a moment nobody says anything, and I watch him through the glass. He's pacing back and forth in front of the shelves. His hair is more rumpled looking than normal, like he's been running his fingers through it. It's kind of cute to see him disheveled, such a rare occurrence.

When I look back at the table, Alice is furiously doodling around the outside of her list. Henry's seat is empty, since he's gone to see Ms. King under the pretense of asking for an extension on a project. In reality we've sent him to investigate Edgar, to poke around and see what we can find out about the new guy.

He has to have vulnerabilities. Soft spots. The more we know about our new enemy, the better.

"We can't prove it because the notes are handwritten," Alice says abruptly. "That's the problem."

I groan, slump into my chair. She's right. I could have written those spells at any time, and he's already performed them. It would be just as easy for him to say I'd seen his spells and attempted to copy them.

"Yeah," Henry says. "And if he changed the snow globe spell just the slightest bit, like we know he did with the dragon, there's no proof it's yours unless you've got it somehow timestamped in that journal of yours."

I shake my head, hating myself for not keeping better records.

The door clicks open, and Oscar tosses his cell phone onto the table. "One cheese, one pepperoni. They'll be here in fifteen." He crosses his arms over his chest and looks at me. "Any ideas?"

"My book only went missing for an hour, at most," I say. I remember the frantic hunt for it, only to find it an hour later, back at the bottom of my locker. I should have known I hadn't just "missed it" in my desperate search. I'd looked in my locker at least three times.

"So how many spells could he have copied in that time?"

I groan, and Alice shakes her head and answers for me. "A lot." She jabs angrily at the page with her pencil. "Doesn't this guy have any spells of his own?"

"Artists create," Oscar says, his gaze still fixed on me, "Hacks rip off."

I can't help feeling a little warm in the face over the compliment, and I give Oscar a quick smile. A second later the door opens again and Henry comes in, slouching his way back over to his chair.

We all look at him expectantly, and he leans forward, elbows on the table, his hands tucked into the sleeves of his sweater. "Okay, so I asked Ms. King. She said Edgar was asking around before he enrolled. Seemed very interested in learning what the highest score at the Spell Writing Championship was last year."

My eyes go wide. "So, he was asking about me."

"Exactly." Henry nods. "Apparently, he'd been accepted into a few schools but he chose this one, because as we know," he spreads his hands wide, "Ms. Lu here has the best score in Washington State."

"So he's a one-upper," Oscar says.

"A what-now?" Alice's pencil is hovering over the paper, like she's about to write down the definition.

Oscar waves impatiently. "The high school I went to, it was filled with these types. Jocks and stuff. The athletes. We called some of them "one-uppers" because there were always a few guys that would compete with one another, and they were ruthless. They'd do almost anything to come out on top."

"So this Edgar guy probably found the school with the highest score," I say slowly, "And then found out the highest scoring student, and then…enrolled here to try to take me down?"

"Probably some rich trust fund prat," Oscar mutters. "But yeah, basically."

"Except that he's less football, and more like a skinny Edgar Allen Poe-wanna be," Alice says, her voice laced with scorn.

I grin at her, feeling a little better about everything. Yeah, he's a spell-stealing jerk, but at least I know what I'm up against now. And I have friends to help me. And on top of that, I think a plan is slowly starting to form at the back of my mind.

Because I am incredibly well acquainted with over-achievers, or "one-uppers" if you want to use Oscar's word. I grew up with a sister who would try to steal my report cards in high school so she could make sure I wasn't getting better grades. One time when she thought I was attracting more attention from boys she put Nair in my shampoo. She was grounded for days.

And now, all I want to do is text her a big thank-you, because I know *exactly* how to deal with Edgar Williams.

These types of people need to be given a taste of their own medicine. You need to utterly destroy them or they'll keep coming at you. And as effective—not to mention dirty—as photocopying pages of my sister's diary was, I doubt the same thing will work on Edgar Williams.

Which is why I've got a new and better plan. It's every bit as dirty, but it's a whole lot bigger this time around.

The next day we begin our campaign. I carry my notebook with me everywhere, and everytime I see Edgar I make sure he seems me writing in it furiously, head down, pen scratching away at the page. My study group does the rest of the work for me. They begin to create rumors, something that Oscar especially seems to delight in. Half the time he's on his phone, texting one person or another, and the other half he makes his way around the school, leaning against one table during lunch, sitting on some girl's desk during free period to whisper in her ear.

At first nothing happens. Edgar just hangs out with his fan club at the end of the hallway, he laughs and flirts, he whispers into the ear of the girl next to him and then grins at her delighted giggles as blue flames race between their hands.

It shouldn't be a big deal really. It's a throw-away spell. A nothing spell. No more than a party trick. But still, I feel like the blue flames are in my stomach, because I've been counting, and that's three so far. Three of my spells he's used blatantly, in front of me.

I could go to the teacher by now, I know that. But it's not enough anymore, not when he looks up, blue fire dancing in his eyes, and smiles at me. He wants me to watch him steal my spells. He wants me to know he's got more.

No, the teachers would simply expel him quietly and without fuss. And that's no longer punishment enough for Edgar Williams. Oh no. I'm going to make sure everyone remembers his name.

When, at last, I start to see people looking at me in the hallway, staring as I pass, I know that it's working.

My study group's message has finally spread. They whisper to one another as I walk by: Aggie is working on a spell, they say. The biggest one yet, they whisper. It's going to blow last year's spell out of the water and win the highest score the Spell Championship has ever seen. Might even be the highest score in the country, who knows.

And finally, finally, it reaches Edgar.

It's a Tuesday morning, and I've shown up early, a Starbucks coffee cup tucked in one arm as I balance my books, heading for the study room.

And there he is, a dark, lanky figure in the middle of the hallway.

I can tell he's heard the rumors because of the way he moves. The way he stands still in the center of the hall, oblivious to the flow of human traffic as everyone moves for their morning classes. The way his eyes fix on me and only me, the hungry light in them. If I didn't have my friends right behind me I'd probably shiver, maybe look away. But instead I feel like I'm facing down a tiger, I feel like a lioness with a pride at her back.

So I meet his gaze and smile.

"Oh, I just got chills," Henry whispers from somewhere behind me, and Oscar mutters,

"Shut up, you just ruined it."

Finally I do turn around, still grinning, feeling a swell of triumph as we make our way to the study room. He totally bought it.

In the weeks that come Edgar Williams does more of my spells. Four more, to be precise. I count every one, taking note, gritting my teeth. There are a few moments when the study group has to talk me down, and one moment in particular when Oscar has to grip my arm to prevent me from launching myself over my desk at the guy—this is when Edgar uses my 'flashlight' spell as a final project in Physical Application of Spell work, to create a glowing sphere of light that he balances on one palm. It only gets worse when he bows his head, still muttering, and creates two more. They flash and shimmer as they

18

rotate in the air above his palms, giving the illusion that he's juggling them, without ever moving his hands. The applause from the class grates on my nerves.

"He keeps adding to them," I mutter to Alice, as we follow in the wake of the class as it spills out into the hall. "He's...he's *perfecting* them."

"No," she says firmly. "They were already perfect. He's just stealing them and adding his own words."

"And he's about to get his comeuppance," Henry adds. "Look."

There it is, the first poster, tacked to the center of the billboard between rideshare notices and signup sheets for after-school writing groups.

The poster for The Spell Writing Championship is obnoxiously bright, purple and yellow stars burst off the page, but all I care about is the date beneath the words.

December 8th – 7:00PM.

Oscar looks over at me. "Are you ready for this?"

I clutch the leather book tightly beneath my arm and bite the inside of my cheek. The poster is like a magnet and I can't look away. The Championship has always been an intense competition. The winner gets a grant, a big one. And there are always at least four or five serious contenders.

But I knew that, it's all part of the plan. In order to win this thing I need to do two things: Create the best spell possible, and take down a thief.

"Yeah," I take a deep breath. "Yeah, I'm ready."

The day of the Championship comes way faster than I want it to, not because I don't have everything ready, I do, but...the rest of me isn't ready for this. Nerves eat at my stomach, and I can't sit still as Henry reads over my spell, checking for errors. I pace back and forth, my boots wearing a path in the thin carpet. I can't stop looking over at him as he reads. He's laid the paper out on the table, smoothing it down with one hand. He's nodding, that's a good sign, right? Why is he narrowing his eyes like that?

Finally, after what seems like forever, he looks up. "This is good," he says slowly. "Aggie, it's *really* good."

The knot in my stomach still doesn't unravel. "Are you sure? Did you check all the commas? Do you think that one beat after the word 'stage' needs—"

"No." Henry points a finger at me, his face the picture of mock-sternness. "Bad, Aggie. No second guessing your genius."

I smile at him in spite of my nerves. "Thanks. I guess I'm just nervous about the competition." My smile dissolves as soon as I say it. What if Edgar doesn't take the bait? What if my plan fails and he creates a spell superior to mine and wins this entire thing?

"You do this every year." Oscar says impatiently. "Of course your spell is genius, but...what about the other thing? Is it all ready?"

"It's ready." I take the paper back from Henry and fold it up carefully, slipping it into the folder I'm taking to the Championship. Then I slide my spell book over to Oscar, feeling my stomach plunge a little. It's taken me weeks to get used to the idea of this. To be so cavalier about my spell book, to risk it this way.

But if this is going to work I have to learn to let it go.

I don't need the book to write my spells, all I need is a pen and paper. I can make magic on an old napkin if I have to.

Oscar flips the book open and scans the page. From the way it sits on the table, upside down, all I can read are the words, "CHAMPIONSHIP SPELL" scribbled along the top of the page. Like all of my other notes, it looks hasty, jotted out quickly, like I did it all in a blaze of inspiration. But I didn't, it's all very carefully copied out to match the rest of the book. To lay out the trap.

I'm purposely late returning to campus after lunch. I'm never late, but this time I very deliberately loiter in my car, nervously telling myself this is all going according to plan. That none of this is insane. This is going to work.

I rush in just as someone is announcing over the PA that Spell Writing For Publication class has been moved to building B.

I can see him out of the corner of my eye, leaning against the radiator at the end of the hall, where he always is. He's watching me, I know that. I curse out loud, ignoring him, shoving my books hastily into my locker before turning around to run back for the staircase.

"Look at Aggie Lu, late for class. I think hell is freezing over as we speak," Edgar calls out, and his obnoxious laughter follows me down the stairwell. But it doesn't even bother me, and as I pelt my way down the steps I can't stop the smile that dances on my lips. Because I know he saw me jam the leather book onto the top of my other books, and I know he saw me "forget" to shut it properly. Three guesses what Edgar Williams is about to do.

The auditorium is packed, every seat filled by friends and relatives—even my parents made it to Seattle today. I spot them in the back row and wave, suddenly nervous.

There's only four of us on stage this year. You have to have a near perfect GPA to even compete. Not surprisingly, Alice stands beside me, and Oscar and Henry are watching from the front row. Both boys give us a thumbs up, and Henry matches his with the cheesiest smile he can manage. That, and the fact that Alice is close enough to reach over and lightly brush my arm with her fingers, makes me feel at least a little less like throwing up.

"You got this," she murmurs. She has to keep her voice way down, because we're grouped close together on stage beneath the brightly shining lights, waiting for our turn at the podium. It's me and Alice on one side of the stage,

Teagan from Advanced on the other, and of course right next to him, Edgar.

Edgar is, hands down, the most arrogant son-of-a-bitch I have ever seen. He keeps looking at me, that's the part that makes this so hard. He stands there with his arms crossed over his chest, head tipped to one side, a smirk on his face. And every so often he shoots me a sideways look.

I wonder what he's thinking.

The book was back in my locker by the time Spell Writing For Publication let out, and I know for sure he took the bait. Not by any magic, but by taking a strand of my hair and tying it around the cover of the book, the same thing I used to do to my diary. If the strand was broken or missing, I knew my sister had read it.

The strand had been missing when I got back to my locker.

So I knew Edgar took the book and looked inside. But the question was, had he taken the bait, or seen through it?

The spell order calls for Teagan first. He steps forward and lifts his hands, tipping his head back slightly so that the lights reflect off his shaggy blond hair. There's no need for any showmanship, not really, the judges don't take points off if you just stand there, but everybody likes a dramatic reading.

The one rule of the Championship is that you have to be able to clean up whatever mess you make, so most of the competitors stick to illusions. Teagan makes his way to the podium, settling his notes on the stand. He spreads his arms and begins to read. Soon the auditorium is full of slowly blooming flowers. The audience claps here, but it's polite clapping, because we've seen this type of thing before, until…he gets to the verses about trees, and suddenly there's a forest all around us, giant oak trees hemming in the stage, appearing behind the rows of seats and between the aisles.

There's a shout of approval from the audience, and more clapping, this time people are impressed. It's a good illusion, I'll give him that. I can actually smell the scent of the forest, pine and fresh air, and hear the faint trickle of a river somewhere.

He'll definitely get points for that.

Next, Alice is up. She turns the stage into the ocean, stretching back as far as you can see. Her spell isn't as flawless as Teagan's, it shimmers and fades here and there, and I can see the audience in their seats past the golden sands of the beach. Still, the smell of salt washes over me, and I give her a big smile as she returns to her place beside me.

She shrugs, struggles to smile back. "Eh, it wasn't as good as I wanted it to be. Knock em dead, Aggie."

The butterflies fluttering in my stomach feel more like poisonous snakes now. I clear my throat. Like Alice, I'm more reserved as I start my spell. There's really no need for flailing limbs, it's not part of magic. However, I do look up from the sheet clutched in my trembling hands from time to time, as I read to the audience.

As I read, the auditorium reshapes itself. The room becomes larger, the roof seems to evaporate into nothing, revealing a stretch of velvet black sky speckled with flecks of shimmering star light. A lagoon lies before the audience, and I am in the middle of it, a sword in one hand, the other still clutching a thin slip of paper in trembling fingers. I am no longer in black slacks and a sweater, but a flowing white dress. It gives me a little thrill, that I can feel a breeze suddenly stir my hair back, that I can almost feel the faint press of cold water around my legs. Almost.

A few people gasp, and then there's the start of applause, but I'm not done yet, I'm still reading, my voice a little stronger than it was before. The sky brightens as the moon comes out, somehow low enough to hang like a huge silver sphere above our heads.

The final paragraph. I lift my empty hand, and though I can see the impression of the sword, it's hard not to grasp my fist as though I'm afraid it will fall out of my trembling fingers. Drops of dark water fly from the end of the blade and hit the front row, and there's a collective gasp.

Then it's over and all at once it's gone, the lagoon, the moonlight, the dress. In one hand my note is clenched in my sweaty fist and the other is empty, though, looking out at the audience, I wish I still had the sword to lift above my head.

There's a burst of applause, so loud I actually stagger a step backwards, and it takes a little while for the auditorium to go quiet again.

When I look over at Edgar he's not smiling anymore. His lips are pressed tightly together, his dark eyes narrow as he stares at me.

I didn't use the spell he'd expected me to. I didn't use the one he was sure he was about to do a better version of. So now he has a choice. He can go ahead with his…my, old spell. Or he can scrap it and try to do something on the fly.

Then he steps up to the microphone, holding a notecard in one hand, and I'm sure he's picked my spell. He darts a sideways look at me, and that smug, superior expression is back on his face. He's going to go ahead with it.

He starts to read, and the auditorium goes quiet.

The spell starts off the way it should. The audience sees a long hallway down the middle aisle, between seats. A door at the end, a key in the palm of his hand…it's always a risky addition, bringing the magician into the illusion like that. I'd already done it on my spell, but I knew it was something he wouldn't be able to pass up.

Edgar raises the key in his hand, still reading.

And that's when the embedded words come in, when he begins to speak the words he doesn't know he's speaking. I tense, and for a moment I feel foolish. Hiding words within words is an old trick, something prose magicians do to prank one another as children. It suddenly seems too simple. Impossible that he won't notice.

But Edgar doesn't notice. He keeps reading.

And something begins to happen in the air above his head, scarlet smoke begins to curl, moving on its own with snake-like twists and turns, until it spells out the word,

Thief

Edgar doesn't look up until the audience starts to murmur, and by then the smoke is already descending, drifting slowly down and down toward him. He steps back, and when it drifts slowly to follow him his eyes go wide.

"What the hell is this?"

I put one hand over my mouth, trying to hide my smile. Edgar rushes across the stage, and the red smoke follows him, reforming over his head to spell the same word whenever he stops. The crowd's muttering is getting louder now, and a few people are laughing. Clearly they've caught on, because no magician would do this to himself.

Edgar is shaking his head now, still backing up, still trying to get out from underneath the red cloud. It dogs him determinedly, and beside me Alice is shaking with silent laughter. In the front row Henry and Oscar aren't even bothering to hide it, they're pretty much howling.

Ms. King rushes up onto the stage. "Oh, uh, folks I guess we're having some technical difficulty with one of our contestants. Mr. Hunter, if you would—ah, perfect thank you."

Mr. Hunter, the Dean of the school, has already rushed onto the stage and begins ushering Edgar off. Edgar only protests for a second, but in that moment he looks back and locks eyes with me, and I smile.

He knows, if he wants it off, he's got to come to the original writer of the spell. And admit he stole it.

Ms. King is speaking into the microphone now, asking that everyone please quiet down and let the judges speak.

The audience goes quiet, everyone focusing on the three judges in the front row seats. There's two men and a woman, all of them solemn faced, like they have absolutely no sense of humor.

They bend their heads together for a few minutes, and the murmur of the audience starts up again, more gentle this time, and drops off when the judges sit up once more.

"After marking everyone for points, taking into account prose and form, and the one gentleman's..." one of the judges, a woman in a pastel business suit pauses, pushing up her glasses, "ahem, disqualification, we have agreed that Ms. Wu is the clear winner, with a score of 95."

Alice seizes me in a hug, and I can barely hear the audience cheering with her yelling in my ear. When I peer over her shoulder I see Henry and Oscar high-fiving in their seats below, and I smile so big it hurts my face.

The next day we're in the study room, grouped around the table. We're doodling on our spells books, laughing and talking when we should be studying, and that's when Edgar finally shows up. He stands in the doorframe, looking particularly sullen. The smoke cloud above his head reforms to spell out thief in bright red, and Oscar snickers.

"That just gets funnier every time I see it." He doesn't flinch when Edgar glares at him, just leans back in his chair and folds his arms over his chest. "Does it say "F=feihT" when you look in the mirror?"

Edgar ignores him. "I want it off," he says, and his voice is a low growl.

Alice tips her head, eyes wide. "Excuse me? I think you better ask our friend that question, but in a nicer tone. In fact, it wouldn't hurt if you got down on your knees and begged a little. You're in no position to demand anything, Mr. Walking Billboard."

Edgar's dark eyes flick to my face. His fists are curled at his sides. "I'm already kicked out of school. They have a zero-tolerance policy."

I don't even bother to smirk at him, but I don't feel bad for him either. He got what he deserved. I slide the

26

folded slip of paper out of my pocket and lean back in my chair, holding it out in his direction. When he shuffles forward the smoke drifts after him and reforms. He snatches the note out of my hand, scowling at me. I think that's going to be it, and I shrug and turn back to my book, when he stops in the doorway.

"What was it?" he says suddenly. "An embedded spell? A spell within a spell?"

"Yeah," I say, keeping my face smooth. "But I made sure to leave the end blank so you could work your...magic."

This time Alice and Henry snicker too, and Edgar gives us one last glare before stomping out of the room.

I stretch back in my chair, and put my hands behind my head, only to find Oscar staring at me. "What?"

"You just have the hugest grin on your face right now." He grins too, apparently thoroughly amused. "Look at Little Miss Nice Guy, kicking ass and taking names."

"I think I could get used to it."

There's another announcement over the PA before Oscar can reply, something about a test this Tuesday, and the four of us groan automatically.

"I guess it's time to stop plotting and start studying," Henry says.

"I'm going to miss the plotting." Alice flips open her text book. "Iambic pentameter is so much less interesting than revenge."

I flip my book open and sit back, listening to Alice complain about poetry. It's back to studying, yeah, but I can't seem to stop smiling.

The End.

E. Latimer is a young adult fantasy writer and literary intern who was born and raised in Victoria, BC and recently moved to Vancouver. Her middle grade gothic fantasy, The Strange and Deadly Portraits of Bryony Gray is coming out from Tundra Books in Spring of 2018. Learn more at elatimer.com

THE LITTLE PINK PSYCHIC SHOP
ANGELA SHELLEY

The little pink psychic shop cozied up alongside Whittier Boulevard, apart from the rest of the strip mall. Shop is generous, shack more accurate, or maybe a shed. It had a presence, a footprint that whispered I am no ordinary building, however small I am.

It was my final journalism project for my final year at Cal State Fullerton. I didn't feel like joining the study group with the police scanner—chasing emergency vehicles just wasn't my speed. So, I picked the weird pink shed down the street from my parent's house to do a community feature story. I'd show the color of the neighborhood, a *How did you end up here* sort of thing.

Inside the dim little room I found the bone rattler. Two-day old beard, salt and pepper but more salt. Keen eye of a realtor sizing me up before the door even closed. But he didn't sell houses, no. He sold lives.

Dusty and ancient as the earth, creaky as a black forest, that man was. Not your usual thing for a strip mall psychic on the better side of town.

"You do palm readings," I asked. "Tarot?"

"Nope." He pulled out his bag of bones. "Back when you were fourteen, you played with a Ouija board."

A slight smile played about his wide, thin lips.

My eyes opened wider and the shadows sidled closer. "Yes?"

"You mightn't've known it, but you unlocked a door to demons with that game. Gave 'em a way to come in and mess with ya." He leaned back in his chair.

"Oh, yeah?" I folded my arms. I didn't believe in demons. Not ones that could harm me, anyway. "Which one?"

Bone rattler went silent for a minute, closed his eyes. "The big one. Satan."

I guess he was right about that too, though I can't be sure anymore.

"Where'd you get those bones?" I asked.

He snorted. "Clients."

He tipped them onto the table, rattling them as they fell. "I can give you what you want, but it'll cost."

"And what do I want?" I asked.

He laughed at that. "Life. The life you dream of."

The bone rattler slid his long fingers down the old yellowing things. "You gonna buy crystals to make sure the devil don't disturb you no more. Two thousand dollars'll do it. I've a man who'll get the geodes, if you got the money."

The sum was almost all I had in my bank account. The money was supposed to go toward a good camera and gas after graduation, while I looked for a placement at a local paper. But you don't want the devil hanging off you like a leech, sucking all the good away, do you? I told him I'd think about it, if I could come back and interview him again. He agreed.

After two weeks of sessions in which I learned very little and gave him even less, he finished reading for me. "You'll see no other psychics again."

"No sir, I won't," I replied.

He rattled his bones. Darkness fell and everything got a little fuzzy.

I left.

Across the parking lot at a table outside Honey Baked Hams, a girl sipped coffee and watched the little pink psychic shop. Curves and earth and life and rich, she was. Not like other girls. Not like the bone rattler.

She was beautiful. A guy like me, more absorbed with news feeds and cameras than footballs, needs every excuse he can get to talk to girls. And I needed another source for my piece.

She put her mug down when I sat across from her.

"I'm Jordan," I said. "I'm writing an article for the college paper."

"That so." She flattened her full, crimson lips and took a drink. Her dark eyes drifted back to the little pink psychic shop.

"Yeah." When I cleared my throat her gaze, green as the glens of Ireland, shot into mine. I pulled out my pad and pen. "Can I interview you?"

She looked at me hard, eyes narrowed. "In exchange for a favor, you may ask me a question."

Hey, she was weird, but dudes will do a lot for a pretty girl's attention. Besides, weird is interesting.

I shrugged, like my heart wasn't racing a mile a minute. "No problem."

"Okay, then. Ask away." She took another drink.

"Have you ever been to that little pink psychic shop?" Sure, it was the most obvious question, but with any interview, you have to start with the basics. Make sure everyone's on the same page.

A pained expression flashed across her face before she glared at the blossom-colored shed. "Nope. But my sisters have."

"And what do you do? Miss…?" My pen held at the ready for her name and number.

"One question, I said." She folded her arms. "It'll be a

31

bigger favor if you want more."

I might forever be indebted to the girl for talking to me. That was acceptable. "Tell me what the favor is, then."

"Get me one of his bones." She took a sip of coffee.

I nodded. Wouldn't be so difficult. I'd ask him for another reading and pocket one of the filthy things. All part of being a journalist and getting her phone number. "And you?"

She sighed. "I'm a witch."

"A witch?" A good journalist puts his judgments away on the job. I wasn't a good journalist, and she looked more economics and cheerleading than candles and midnight rituals in the woods.

I plastered my most charming smile on and held out my hand. "I've never met a witch before."

"Yep. I'm Nix." She frowned and didn't offer hers.

Okay, then. I turned back to my notepad and scratched down *witch, doesn't shake hands.* "What kind are you? What do you... do?"

"My gift is in the living earth, Gaia." Another sip.

"And your sisters are your... sorority?" I couldn't shake the thought that she belonged in a study group, cramming for an exam.

"*Coven* is the word you're looking for." Nix stared unbroken at the Little Pink Psychic Shop. "He has them, all six. I need his bones to take his power and call them back."

I sucked in a breath of air, chilled.

She rubbed her arms. "I can protect you, if you get the bones."

"I want to go home, first." That cold climbed into my heart like it'd been years since I'd been home, since I'd been warm. I needed a shower and dinner.

"Of course," Nix said with a sympathetic look. She fished in her large gold purse that hung from the table by one of those jeweled hook things. "Keep this on you. With it, I can connect to you."

I slipped a rough little pouch filled with herbs, beads, and God-knows-what into my pocket.

"There's one more thing," she said, placing her hand next to mine.

"Yes?" I shivered at her closeness. Maybe she'd come on a date after this. For a second, I let myself believe it possible.

"With this, you'll be able to bring back one item. Something that belonged to you, something you gave him. Bring it and he'll never have power over you again. I'll make sure of it. You'll be free."

Free. Why did she think I needed freedom? What did I need to be free of? Goosebumps prickled my spine, answers hovered just out of reach.

"Why me?" I asked. "Why aren't *you* doing this?"

Nix gave me a sad smile. "The bone rattler got *six* of my sisters, each coming to save the last. My entire coven. I cannot be the seventh. You're the only one he won't suspect. You're the only one who can do this."

I went to my folk's place, showered, and typed up my notes. Mom and Dad weren't home, no big surprise. I couldn't shake the feeling that the place felt different, filled with echoes of the past. I longed to stay, but felt pulled back to the little pink psychic shop. Back to Nix.

Those bones were from his clients, the rattler admitted it himself. Nix's sisters, were they prisoners? Dead? Did Nix want their remains to give them a proper burial?

I should go to the cops, I thought. But if *I* broke the story of a local murderer—a serial one too—I wouldn't just get an A in my investigative reporting class. I'd get a job at the LA Times.

When I arrived at the strip mall, Nix was still drinking coffee at Honey Baked Hams and watching the little pink psychic shop from a distance.

The bone rattler was still there too.

"Ah, you've returned," he said, smoothing the velvet bag. "Did you enjoy your time away?"

I sat across from him, his long obsidian glass table between us. "I have more questions for my article."

"Do you now." It wasn't a question. He steepled his fingers on the cold black surface.

"What powers do you claim to have?" I readied my pen and paper for a confession.

A corner of his mouth lifted, ever so slightly. He'd indulge me, I knew, while leading me into a greater web.

"You should be able to guess, I imagine." With slow deliberation, he rattled the bones and cast them. "I have power over the dead."

Wind whistled around the shed. Within the sound flew words, light and musical, earthen and rich. Nix saw that hawk-eyed man, and she called up forces from the depths of the seas, from the thunder in the sky. The bone rattler's frown deepened into a scowl.

"The littlest sister sent you, did she?" he sneered and gathered up his divination. One piece clattered to the floor.

Outside of my volition, I nodded.

"No matter." The bone rattler stood and crossed to the middle of the shed, lifted a rug, and opened a seamless hatch in the wood-paneled floor. "You shall come, young Jordan, and she will follow."

He thought he'd catch her, a goddess for himself. But she was no fool. No bones could bar the life in Nix. He had nothing to shackle her, no demons to bargain with.

With his sweeping motion, I lifted from the chair and was dragged down rough-hewn stairs in the rock. But before plunging into darkness, I grasped the slender white bone under the table.

In that darkness, candles flickered.

In that darkness, bones lined the walls.

In that darkness, I had no body.

"I'm… am I…?" I grasped at words I could not utter

as I felt for my body. It wasn't there.

"Dead?" The bone rattler chuckled. "Yes, my dear boy. You've been for quite some time. And you've grown indispensable to me. Almost."

"But. How?" Cold chilled me through.

The bone rattler made a face and shrugged. "How do any of these things happen, I say. It's the way of the universe. Life and death. Death and life. One follows the other."

And there, across the way, my eyes fell on something familiar. My journalist's pad, half buried in the dirt. The image of the notebook in my hand flickered. The skeleton propped against the wall beside it wore darkened shreds of my clothes. Its left hand was gone.

"Me." I fell before the thing that was no longer myself. "Me."

Words whispered in my ear. *It's me, Jordan. Nix. Help me.*

The bone rattler busied himself with a massive stone bowl and a shelf of powders and liquids. He hummed happily. "And thanks to you, my lad, soon I'll have the seventh star. Seven goddesses to do my bidding. My powers will be complete."

Nix was above, somewhere. I felt her in the sky, in the earth, the walls around me, the core of the metallic heart spinning below us. She was as vast as he, or more so. She whispered to the depths of my soul.

Find my sisters and you'll be free.

Six girls. Somewhere down here, I had to find Nix's six sisters. My determination felt paper-thin, thinner than the vaporous existence I held. Steel rested in bones a world and lifetime away, but it was steel nonetheless. For Nix, for myself, for everything I was once, I'd do this. I'd find them.

Roots gathered around my feet, at my back, around my arms, pulling me into the earth. I stepped into it when the bone rattler turned his back, and gave myself to the soil.

Around me clung darkness and the heat of the earth.

Around me gathered energy and life. Around me filled with chanting and song. I followed.

Moments later those roots pushed me into a new space. A cavern, almost. A grave. Blacker than black. Silent save for the hushed breath of six young women huddled together.

You'd think at a moment like this, I'd have something heroic to say. Apparently not. "Um, are you okay?"

A gasp.

"Who's there?" a small, weak voice replied.

"Jordan," I said, approaching them carefully. One still sang the whispered melody that drew me to them. "Nix sent me."

Mixed cries of relief came.

"Here." One struggled to move, another scratched at the wall.

"Take this to her." An outstretched hand held a small pouch, very much the same as the one given me. I put it in my pocket next to the other.

"Do you have one for me?" the girl asked. "One from Nix?"

"Oh. She said..." I didn't have the heart to tell them that Nix's pouch was for me, not them. Or was it for me at all?

A third voice broke, coughed out a laugh. "She sent him without one. That's so Nix."

"No, no. She gave me one," I blustered. "It's just... she told me to use it for myself."

A sigh. A fourth girl, silent until now, wept.

"Fine," the one who gave me the pouch said. "Take ours to her, take your bones, and be free. If we're lucky, she can figure out what to do with mine."

"But Asia..." the second said. "The connection will be too weak. We're too far."

"I *know*," Asia hissed. "Don't you think I know? But that's the deal she made with him. Into the earth, find us, and be released from the bone rattler."

36

The six girls began to chant, and again the earth pulled me.

"Bring her my talisman," Asia said as I drew away. "And be free."

I drew about half-way into the soil, and got stuck.

"Well, go." Asia spat out the words, angry again.

Someone murmured a different sound, and light spilled into the little cave. Around us the roots of a great tree glowed in hues of blue, purple, and gold. Before me sat six young women, smudged in dirt but beautiful. Stunning, really. Mahogany skinned, alabaster tones, and all between, with eyes of earth and sky and forest.

"Why aren't you going?" Asia asked.

"I'm stuck." Heat turned my ears red. Or what would have been my ears, if I had any.

"He's carrying too much," whispered the second girl. "He's too bound to the bone rattler."

The earth around me sighed as the others stopped the chant.

Asia closed her bronze-lidded eyes and rubbed her temples. "Let me think. We can figure this out—"

But there was only one way. I pulled Nix's pouch from my pocket, placed it on the cavern's dirt floor, and went into the earth.

Nix's song drew me back. Back to the sun, the light, the skin of the mother.

I placed Asia's pouch on her table. It was caked in soil and something darker.

"Thank you." Nix choked as she pulled the pouch to her chest. She rubbed a tear from her eye and looked into mine. "I'm going to go. I should be able to find them, now. You're free, too."

I shook my head. "I'm not. I had to leave your pouch behind."

Nix's cheeks paled.

I dropped the bone onto the table. "I could only bring this." My non-existent stomach turned. "I think it's the meta-tarsal from my ring finger."

Nix clutched it, and I felt warm all over. "Then you're coming with me, too."

I got my date. I smiled for the first time that I could remember. "So, your place, then?"

Nix rolled her chocolate eyes and walked to a sunshine-yellow beater of a car. She sat and started the engine, and I pulled myself into the seat beside her. I'd never been able to leave the little pink psychic shop without the bone rattler's permission before. She brushed my cheek, or where it would've been.

"You know, you were kind of cute." A corner of her mouth lifted as she put the car in gear and drove away. "Let's go get my sisters."

Angela Shelley is the award-winning author of the fantasy series Ennara. She spends her days in Los Angeles wrangling twin Scorpios and writing adventures with magical heroines and time-travelling rogues. Learn more at angelashelley.net

SOMETHING NEW
ELIZA BOYD

Chapter 1

Erin

"Remind me to never transfer schools again." I toss the last box on my bed and grab the phone from between my ear and my shoulder. "Unpacking is such a nightmare."

"But it's a fresh start, E!" Roxie reminds me. "New classes, new scenery, new friends. Maybe even new boys…" She's likely raising her eyebrows and grinning like a fool.

I sigh, propping a hand on my hip. "Don't even start. That's the absolute last thing I need."

"Oh, you don't start," my friend throws back at me. "A breakup doesn't mean you should close yourself off forever."

While walking over to the kitchen, I huff out a breath. I get it. I really do. And it won't be for the rest of eternity. But… "I'm not ready."

"You've been saying that for months, E. At some point, you're going to have to—"

"I know," I say, interrupting her. More quietly, I add,

"I know, okay? Just..." I look around my new studio apartment, searching as if the right words will write themselves on the wall somewhere. "Not right now. One thing at a time."

It takes her a few moments, but she finally relents. After a deep sigh, she says, "Fine. One thing at a time. Go rock at school like you normally do."

That puts a smile on my face. If there's one thing I'm good at, it's school. Or being awkward, but that's not something I'm nearly as proud of.

"And go check out Tempe. It may not be *your* thing," she says, and I can picture her pointing a finger at me, "but ASU is rather known for its parties, so enjoy yourself. None of this 'all work and no play' garbage just because you don't want a boyfriend, okay?"

"Fine, Mom," I laugh through the phone. Then, while Roxie giggles too, I lean forward and place my elbows on the kitchen counter. "I'll talk to you later. I'm going to try to unpack now."

"Ugh," she moans. "Good luck with that. You know I'd help, but..."

I let out a sharp laugh. "Seeing as you're eighteen hundred miles away, that was a hollow offer at best." But I smile too. "Thanks, Rox. I miss you, ya know."

"I miss you more, and I know you know that." There's a quiet second, and then she says, "But I also know that you have to do what you have to do. And you'll get there. I know you will. The free spirit is strong in you."

All I can do is shake my head. She's not wrong.

"Call me if you need anything. And don't do anything I wouldn't do," she tells me. Then she bursts out laughing and hangs up.

I shake my head and stare at my phone like I can't believe she did that. Even though I totally can. Oh, how I'll miss seeing her every day.

That's Roxie in a nutshell though. She's pretty much my opposite in every way—kooky, outgoing, willing to try anything once. I may have a free spirit, but it doesn't guide me too many different ways.

Except, well, to a new college on the other side of the country. But ya know.

I cross my arms on the counter and let my head fall forward. Like she said, I have to do what I have to do. And I had to get far, far away from all reminders of the past. I needed a fresh start. A place where no one knows who I am and I can recreate myself, be whoever I want. New classes. New scenery. New friends.

And…maybe even new boys.

But I'll worry about that later. Right now, it's all about unpacking and figuring out my new space. And ignoring the fact that I should be much more worried about being alone in every sense of the word for the first time in my life. And trying to locate a knife to cut these boxes open.

Oh shoot. I left that last bag of stuff—the one with my box-opening knife, which I was smart enough not to put into a taped-shut box—in my car. So I snatch my keys off the counter. I nearly put my coat on, but then I remember that Phoenix Valley winters are basically Indiana spring temperatures, so I skip that and then head out the door.

As soon as I open my car door, I spot the bag. Right there on the front seat. Roxie's phone call must have distracted me. I toss the bag over my shoulder and close the door.

On my way back to my apartment, I pass a bulletin board full of flyers, posters, and other advertisements of the goings-on around campus. Arizona State University is a massive school, so I doubt I'll have trouble staying busy—a.k.a. staying distracted from real life. Lord knows I have some major issues to work through. But I'd rather not yet. Like I told Roxie: One thing at a time. This new environment is the one thing at the moment.

Luckily, something right up my alley catches my eye. A bright-green piece of paper has all the details I need to start my final college semester off right.

Chapter 2
Eli

Walking is one of my favorite things. Well, it usually is. It's not that much fun when you're carrying a stack of extra posters and the sun is unusually hot for this time of year. Luckily, I can use them to block the sun, but I'd like to save some upper-body strength for when it comes time to hold my poster up. I don't want to have to use it during the two-mile walk to the protest.

Oh well. We all make choices, and this one is mine.

I know a lot about choice. My brother, Jake, has taught me a few lessons over the years. So I don't take choice lightly.

Like, right now, I could choose to call someone and ask for a ride. Unfortunately, no one I know from campus is going to this event. I've met a few people in the last two months at events like these, but none of them go to ASU with me, and I'm not great at reaching out for help— which is another thing I got from my brother. So I trudge along in the afternoon sun. The cause is worth it.

What's not worth it is knocking someone over due to my inability to see with these posters obstructing my line of sight. Whoops. I drop the posters in an effort to save whoever I nearly ran over. As they scatter all across the sidewalk, I shoot my arms out to keep her from falling. I'm almost too late, but I swoop in in the nick of time.

"Whoa! Sorry!" I pull her to me to steady her and keep her upright. But, instead of letting her go and making sure she's okay, we...stay like this.

Her cheek pressed against my chest. My arm curled around her waist. Her hands splayed on my back. My hand resting on her hair.

And we take a few seconds to just breathe.

I breathe in the scent of her hair, which reminds me of a tropical island, though I've never been to one. She takes a huge breath too, which expands her chest and presses her closer to me. Which I take advantage of by inhaling her yet again.

When she finally raises her head to peek up at me, she seems to gather herself and realize that what we're doing isn't normal for two people who've never met before. So she scrambles away and looks around near her feet. Though I don't miss the pink on her cheeks.

"What are you looking for?" I ask so I can help her.

She spins in a circle, her gaze on the ground. "My sign..." She trails off, putting a finger to her lips, and then bends to pick through the ones I dropped. "It fell when we collided."

Her sign? All I see are mine littering the sidewalk.

After she has flipped a few over, I kneel to help her. But I don't know what I'm looking for. And I almost don't want to ask, because if we find it, then our time together will be over.

"What's on yours?" I pick one up, but it's one of mine.

"It says—oh!" she exclaims as she snatches one from the ground. Her eyes light up, and her smile hits me right in the gut. "Here it is!"

One look at her poster tells me that we're headed to the same place. And the car keys sticking out of her back pocket might give me the chance to make a better choice for myself.

Whether that's a better choice because I don't want to walk or because I can be around her longer, I don't know. I don't even think I care.

"Looks like we used the same poster board," I tell her, wanting her to make the connection that our destinations are the same.

"Looks like we're both going to the same protest, huh." She grins again and holds her sign with just her left hand. With her right hand, she shields her eyes from the sun. "I'm Erin, but my friends call me E."

"So, which one should I call you?" I hope I get to call

her E. I'd love for us to start off as friends. And it's not lost on me how similar her nickname is to what my brother calls his wife.

"Don't get ahead of yourself, dude." Her eyes sparkle in the sunlight that sneaks past her fingers. "I'm brand new here and don't need to get in with the wrong crowd. I'm sure you understand."

I smirk at her. "Oh right. You mean those crazy people who hold up signs on street corners to bring awareness to injustice and cruelty?" Shaking my head, I say, "Definitely don't get mixed up with them." Then I wink. Like I'm my brother or something.

But her giggle is worth it. "Yeah. Those nutjobs." She laughs a little harder and glances at her poster. "Damn them for trying to change the world for the better."

Her fist-shake at the sky turns my smirk into a full smile.

When she's done laughing, she sighs. "Actually, is there any chance you could help me get there? I meant what I said about being new here."

I give a small chuckle and bend to pick my posters up. "And don't you need to know the name of the man you're asking to take you there?" From the ground, I look up at her.

The sun on her hair makes her blond curls shine like a halo. The hand on her hip as she squints at me lets me know how much trouble I am in. Apparently, she's part attitude and part angel. And, especially from this position, I'm at her mercy.

She waits until I'm back at my full height, with my signs back in my hands, before she speaks. "What do people who aren't your friends call you?"

I shrug. "That's anyone's guess, isn't it?" Then I cock an eyebrow. "But you"—I narrow my eyes and point a finger at her—"can call me E."

"Oh, I can?" she laughs. "Is your name Erin too?"

"No, it's Eli," I tell her. "Which is what my friends call

me. But, with you, I think E will do just fine."

She scrunches her face up in an adorable way. With a smirk, she says, "We'll see about that," before spinning around and taking her keys out of her pocket. When she clicks a button on the fob, her car beeps and the headlights blink.

I stare after her, unable to move as this surprising woman walks away from me. After a few moments, I shake the stupor off and realize I better chase after her. Though we will likely end up at the same place, I feel drawn to her. Like I might be chasing after her for the rest of my life if I don't act now.

With all of my signs in my hand, I stop at her passenger's side door. With her door open, she looks at me over the top of her car.

"I have the directions and a lot of signs to carry, E. I'll help you get there."

She opens her mouth to say something—likely another smartass comment I'll love—but she closes her mouth instead. Then, after a single nod, she gets in the car. And I follow her.

Because I might go wherever she'll lead.

Chapter 3
Erin

February in Arizona is much like January in Arizona—but it's a little warmer. And that's a lot different than February in Indiana. It's actually snowing back home right now. I thought I'd miss that, but apparently, twenty frigid winters is enough for me. I think I can tolerate this gorgeous sunshine for a while.

School is also a lot different here than it was in Indiana, and I'm thankful for that. There are more people at this school than there are in my hometown. No one here cares about why I'm here as much as the people in my small farm town do. And I seem to have found my people. No one back home understood me or my choices. But they are mine to make.

Which includes breaking off a six-year relationship with the guy I thought I was going to marry.

People change. Sometimes, people become different than they used to be. And, sometimes, that's good. But, other times, that's not. And that was the case with me and Derek.

"Really?" Eli asks while leaning his elbows on my kitchen counter. "You up and left right before the start of this semester because you two broke up?"

I shake my head, ready to explain the story again. But then I stop, stir the pasta in the pot a little, and nod instead. "Yeah. Pretty much."

"Huh." He blinks at me a few times. "Just like that."

"Just like that," I repeat. "I looked at him and suddenly didn't recognize him anymore. We had both turned into incredibly different people, and our morals weren't lining up. So I made a choice."

"A few of them, it seems." He stands up straight and heads to the fridge.

To his back, I raise an eyebrow. In the past month, we've gotten to know each other. Mostly through attending protests together—the Phoenix area isn't short on opportunities, thankfully—but also through some quiet moments where it's just the two of us. I've grown to trust him. And it's nice to have someone I can rely on when everything I've ever known is almost two thousand miles away.

Right. Simply someone to rely on. That's what I'll keep telling myself about Eli. That's what I'll say instead of acknowledging the fluttery feeling I get in my belly when he knocks on my door or texts me to see if I got to class okay. Sure. We'll go with that.

"What's that supposed to mean?" I ask him as he pours the spaghetti sauce into a microwave-safe bowl.

He turns the burner off and takes the pot over to the

sink to drain the noodles. "Just that you made some choices really quickly."

"Roxie says that the free spirit is strong in me." I smile at the microwave while the sauce warms up.

"Hmm." He brings the noodles back to the stove, and when the microwave beeps, he adds the sauce to the pot of noodles.

I squint at him. "And what's *that* supposed to mean?" Leaning against the counter, I cross my arms over my chest.

He shakes his head. Because he's spent most of his time with me lately, I have no idea when he got a haircut last. Seems to me like it's longer than he likes it, but I kind of appreciate the length to it. As in I kind of want to run my fingers through it.

But, obviously, I don't.

"I guess I just don't understand snap decisions like that," he explains. "I could never leave my family because of a breakup."

"We come from totally different places." I push off the counter and cross to the fridge. "And I didn't ask you to understand. I just felt ready to tell you, E."

At that, he stops stirring our dinner. His shoulders fall as he lets out a deep exhale. "You're right," he says. "Thank you for sharing that with me."

To the back of his thin frame, I say, "Thank *you* for basically being my only friend here."

"It's a good thing I like spending time with you," he mumbles under his breath, smirking at me over his shoulder.

I don't say anything for a while. Too long. Because he glances over at me and winks before stirring the pasta with the sauce one last time. And there go those fluttery stomach flips again. So I take a deep breath and clear my head.

I meant what I said to Roxie. I wasn't ready, and I'm still not ready. I'm happy to have a friend here in Arizona.

Even if this friend is someone I'd like to be more than friends with. The problem lies in the fact that I've had only one boyfriend so far in my life, so I have no idea how to be with someone else. Again, my free spirit has its limits. But that's okay. Spending time with Eli is more than enough right now. Because, like I said, I'm not ready.

The pasta *is* ready, though, so I reach toward the cabinet to get bowls. But, as he reaches at the same time, our fingers brush. Both of us freeze, our arms outstretched, our fingers on the stack of bowls we're both aiming for. I want to be the first to move—I *should* be the first to move. But I'm stuck, wishing that more than just our fingers were touching.

Honestly, I don't know how much longer I'll be able to ignore these feelings. Especially when they're happening so frequently.

Eli clears his throat and drops his hand first. Then he steps back and puts that hand in the pocket of his jeans before going back to stir the pasta. Because, obviously, it desperately needs to be stirred right now. Yep. I should have thought of that.

Instead, I'm still standing with my hand on the bowls like an idiot. I finally shake myself out of that weird trance and remove two bowls from the cabinet. He did say that he likes spending time with me. Does he like it like *that*? No, we're just friends, right? But, if we're just friends, what was that weird moment we just had?

Ugh. I don't know. And I should focus on school, not what could be between me and my only real friend here. It doesn't matter that I've been here for a month and could have made other friends. Eli's the only one I really want or need. If I'm lonely without him, I call Roxie. That's good enough for me.

But Eli—he's gone to this school for four years. Yet I haven't seen him hang out with many other people. And we do see each other every day now—

"Here you go," he says, holding a bowl of spaghetti out

to me and breaking me out of my thoughts.

I blink, shake my head, and take the bowl from him. "Thanks," I mutter before heading to the table with my food.

He doesn't ask me if I'm okay. He doesn't ask me what that was about. And he doesn't ask me if I want more of my favorite tea with my dinner. He just gets the tea out of the fridge and takes his usual seat right next to me.

Where we pretend we're not both feeling something one of us isn't ready for. Something one of us shouldn't even want, considering I'll likely be back in Indiana when the school year is over. And the other person... Well, I don't know. And that's only half the problem.

Chapter 4
Eli
"When's your flight?" I ask Erin as I scoop my backpack over my shoulder.

"Yeah... About that..." She trails off, spinning around to head out the door with me.

I lock the door behind us and squint at her. "What about it? It's spring break, so when are you leaving?"

She wrings her hands in front of her, twisting until the tips turn red. "Well, actually," she starts slowly, "I'm not." Her smile at the end is fake. Fake as hell.

I'm practically an expert when it comes to her facial expressions at this point. We've spent the last two and a half months nearly glued to each other's sides. Which has been great for getting to know her. But it hasn't been so great for my ailing heart. It beats too hard and too erratically when she's near me. Yet it doesn't beat as enthusiastically when she's not, so I don't know which side to be on.

Crossing my arms over my chest, I say, "Then what are you doing?"

I should know—for the same reason why I know how

fake her smile is. But I don't. How could I possibly not know this? I think back, but I guess we never really talked about our plans. I assumed she'd go back to Indiana and be with her family, which is probably why I never asked. The last thing I've wanted to think about is a week without my best friend.

Apparently, she's not doing that.

She shrugs. "I'm just gonna stay here, probably eat at Loving Hut and Green a whole bunch of times." Again, she lifts her shoulders and lets them fall. "No big deal. I'll see you when you get back."

"Uh, no," I tell her, putting my second backpack strap on my other shoulder. "That's ridiculous."

With narrowed eyes, she stares me down. "Excuse me?"

I wasn't expecting that reaction, and then I realize I went a little caveman on her. Seems like my brother and I have more in common than I thought. Over the years, I've seen the way he's been with Diana. And he practically raised me, so I guess the apple doesn't fall far from the tree.

"Sorry." I glance at the ground, not wanting to make her uncomfortable by demanding things from her.

We still haven't clarified what's really going on between us, but I won't push it until I can tell she's ready for that. So far, she isn't, but that doesn't mean I feel great about leaving her alone for a week in a town she's otherwise alone in. And, if I push, she might make a crazy snap decision. Which always has me second-guessing myself and what to do about my feelings for her.

Push her too far too fast and I might never see her again. She might transfer schools in the middle of the semester just to get away from me.

When I look at her again, I clear my throat. "I think you should come with me."

Again, she repeats, "Excuse me?" This time, though, her eyes are wide. "I should go with you? Where are *you* going?"

"To my brother's house. And I'll probably see my dad while I'm there too." I start walking toward the parking lot of my complex—where Erin's car is.

As she rushes to catch up with me, she says, "You think I should go to your brother's house with you? For a week?"

I nod as we walk.

"Will they have somewhere for me to sleep?"

I almost tell her that my room there has a bed big enough for both of us, but that won't fly with her. Instead, I nod again. Lissa, my twin sister, won't be home, so she can crash in there.

"Can we still eat at Loving Hut and Green?" she asks when we get to her car.

At that, I crack a smile and laugh a little. Her priorities are in the right place—food's hugely important to me and my family too. She'll fit right in.

"Yep. Though I bet we can get my brother to cook for us too."

She rests her arms on top of her car and stares at me for a few beats—probably asking herself if this is a good idea. Going back home with me to meet my family? What could possibly go wrong?

Finally, she sighs. "It sounds better than being without…" She suddenly stops and corrects herself. "Better than being alone all week." Then she rushes out with, "I need to stop at my place and get some clothes."

I think she was about to say that it sounds better than being without *me*, but I won't let my heart hope for that. Instead, I nod. "Of course." Because I don't have to hope for anything. She's coming home with me. Not going back to Indiana. That's all I need right now.

"Hi!" Carissa squeals when she opens the door. She wraps her small arms around me and squeezes me with her unusually strong grip. "I've been waiting all day for you to come home!"

Technically, she's my step-niece, I guess. My brother's wife's daughter. But she's more like a little sister to me. And she's all the good things about coming home.

"Carissa! You don't have to squeeze him to death," Diana says as she comes around the corner with baby Liam on her hip. She freezes for a second to get a good look at me. "Are you growing your hair out?" But she completely stops short when she gets an eyeful of Erin. "Oh, hey there. I'm sorry. Eli didn't mention he was bringing someone home." Then she gives *me* an eyeful.

"This is Erin." I try to stress her name so she understands where I'm going with this, but she looks at me like she doesn't. Even though I know she does. "My *friend* from school," I add with even more emphasis.

"She's really pretty," Carissa tells me.

All I can do is nod and soak in the awkward weirdness that's descended upon us.

Erin breaks the tension by reaching a hand forward. "Hi. You're Diana, right? Eli's told me a lot about you guys."

"Likewise," Diana responds, shaking Erin's hand and holding Liam tighter to her with one arm.

That earns me a raised-eyebrow glance from Erin.

I shrug at her, taking my nephew from Diana's arms. "You're always at my place. What else am I going to talk about when my family calls?"

It's small, but I don't miss that slight smile that curves her full lips. And it seems Diana doesn't miss that I didn't miss it. So another round of awkward weirdness takes us over.

Luckily, my brother shouts from the kitchen. "I can't leave the stove! Come here and say hi."

With the tension broken, I almost sigh with relief. Until my brother continues speaking, that is. And he embarrasses the shit out of me.

"Get in here so I can meet your girlfriend."

Chapter 5
Erin
"I can't believe you have to leave already!" Diana gives me a big, warm hug around her growing belly. "It's been really great getting to know you, Erin."

When she holds me at a distance and gives me a long look, goose bumps break out over my skin. I've fallen in love with Eli's family, and I can't believe we have to go already, either. I could stay in this house, with all of its love and respect, forever. Everyone has been amazing, even Eli's father. I'd thought that that would've been weird, but it wasn't. They all have their place in the family, and they fit together really well. It's a shame I have no real excuse to come back whenever I want to.

"I'm sure she'll come back to visit us," Jake says, holding his son in his arms. "Right, little man? Tell Erin she's always welcome here." He points Liam's little hand at me for emphasis.

Diana puts one hand on her belly and the other on her husband's arm. The love between the two of them is clear as day, and I can only hope to have something like that in my life. So I smile at them, enjoying being among people who care so deeply for each other. But Eli's turning shades of red I've never seen on a human being before.

"Can we stop embarrassing me, please?" He slings his backpack over one shoulder and opens the front door. Then he grabs my bag and heaves it over his other shoulder. "I'll be in the car, E."

With her elbow, Diana nudges Jake in the ribs. She stares at Eli with wide eyes as he leaves. "Did you hear that?" she loudly whispers to him.

Before I can ask what in the world she's talking about, my phone buzzes in my back pocket. So I reach into it to see who's calling me. When I see Roxie's name on the screen, I decide to take the call.

Waving at Jake and Diana, I say, "Thanks so much again for having me." Then I hold my phone out for them to see, point out the door with my thumb, and start following Eli to the car.

He already has our bags in the trunk by the time I make it to the driver's side door. As I open it, I answer the phone.

"Hey," Roxie says hesitantly.

Alarm bells go off. Lots of them. Roxie's never hesitant. She's purposeful and unapologetic. So what the heck is wrong? I ask her as much while I put my seat belt on with one hand.

"Well, are you sitting down?" she asks.

I look over at Eli, who's looking at me like he wants to take the phone from me. "I am. I just got in the car."

"Oh. Where are you going?"

"Back home," I tell her.

"From?" she asks, not missing a beat.

"Eli's house," I answer as I start the car. Too late, I realize my mistake.

"Oh snap. At eleven in the morning? What have you been up to, girl?"

I peek over at Eli. He's laughing to himself—likely because he heard what Roxie said. Unlike me, he's not mortified that she thinks our relationship is something it's not. Yet I don't know if I'm mortified because she thinks it is or because it's not when I want it to be.

Honestly, it doesn't matter though. He pulls back any time we touch. I lost count of how many times he insisted to his family that we're "just friends." And he's right: I should have gone back home this week. I should have been with *my* family—not his. But I can't find it in me to be sorry that I spent spring break with the Reynolds family.

"Hey, Roxie," Eli says loud enough for her to hear through the phone. He doesn't deny her accusation, but he doesn't confirm it, either.

So we sit in awkward silence until Roxie clears her throat down the line.

"Right. What's up?" I ask her.

"Oh, yeah. That. So…"

I could strangle her. What in the hell is going on? "Spit it out, Rox. I'd like to get back home—"

"Derek is seeing someone," she says in a rush.

Well, that shuts me up. In all the time I've been here, I haven't thought much about Derek. Which is a shock, considering I'd spent much of the last six years thinking about him. I guess I haven't had much time to let him take my thoughts over. So I certainly haven't wondered what it'd be like when he moved on.

"Someone we've never met. And not just that," Roxie continues.

"Oh, god," I groan. "There's more?"

"Yes—the part you should be sitting down for."

"Well, I'm sitting. So lay it on me," I tell her.

"He's kind of"—she drags the words out in a way so unlike her, and I start sweating—"having a baby with her."

Whoa. That was…well, not at all what I was expecting.

All the air leaves my lungs in a loud *whoosh*. My heart starts pounding, and my world goes silent. I nearly drop my phone, but I somehow keep it by my ear.

I'm not sure if Eli heard what she said or just knows exactly how I need him and what I need him to do, but he gets out of the car, comes over to the driver's side, and scoots me over to the passenger's seat. It's no easy task, and I'm barely mindful of the movement. But the next thing I know, I'm on the right side of the car, Eli's backing out of his brother's driveway, and Roxie's trying to get my attention.

And Eli's hand goes to mine as soon as the car is in drive.

That's what brings me back to reality. My best friend. My anchor. My…something else I can't possibly name in this life-altering moment.

"You there, girl?"

I finally understand English again, so I respond with, "Yeah." Then I have to clear my throat. "I'm here. Wow."

"Yeah, I know. But I wanted you to hear it from me because I don't think he's about to call you up and tell you. I didn't want you to read about it on Facebook or something stupid."

"Okay. Yeah. Thanks, Rox." Then I hang up and drop my phone, not caring where it lands.

Eli squeezes my hand and brings our intertwined fingers to his lap. There, his warmth soothes my rattled nerves in a way Roxie's words can't. And he keeps his grip on my hand the entire silent, half-hour drive back to school.

I'm glad I got the news from Roxie, and I'm glad I'm getting this out of the way. Eventually, I was going to hear about how Derek had moved on. Yet I can't help but think how much worse this would have been if I'd been alone when she'd told me.

Scratch that. It's not just that I'm not alone. This would have been much worse if I hadn't been with Eli. If I'd been with anyone else, I'd have fallen apart. Because hearing that the man I was going to marry is having a baby with someone when we broke up only late last year... That should have destroyed me. And I won't lie and say I'm not crushed.

But having Eli by my side, holding my hand—that's making all the difference.

Chapter 6
Eli

I knock on her door at nearly midnight. No, I don't care that it's this late on a weeknight and we both have class in the morning. She's been ignoring my calls and my texts for the last four days, ever since we got back from spring break. And I've waited as long as I can for her to come to me. This separation ends now.

After the week we had with my family, I'd thought things had changed a little. We've both shared more stuff with each other—her stories about her past, my home life with my family. But that open door slammed shut the second she got that devastating phone call from Roxie.

I dropped her off at her place with an offer to do whatever I could to help her out. I was fully prepared to listen to her go on and on about her ex if that's what it was going to take. But she never took me up on it. Maybe showing up right now would seem a little too forward to her, but not having her in my life has been harder than I'd thought it'd be. It's time I use my power of choice for myself. So here I am.

Knocking. And waiting. And knocking some more.

Good thing she doesn't have a roommate.

Finally, after approximately three million knocks, she swings the door open. "E? What are you doing here? It's so late." She rubs her eyes and shades them from the light over her front door.

Even with sleep-mussed hair and lines on her cheek from her pillow, she's gorgeous. Every cell in my body lights up with awareness when I'm around her, and right now is no different. I can't continue to deny what I feel for her, so I choose now to start showing her.

Nothing over the top though. I just wrap my arms around her and give her a hug. It's something best friends would do, but I hold on to her a little longer than is necessary.

"I've just missed my friend and thought I'd check on her," I tell the top of her head. "How's it going?"

"I needed some time by myself," she says into my chest. "To deal and process."

I can understand that, so I give her a small squeeze. "And how's that been going for you?"

When I take a big breath, I get a whiff of the same

scent from the day we ran into each other. The day when I held her almost like this and didn't want to let go. Though I'm glad I did, if only so I didn't scare her, I'm also glad I still get to see her on a regular basis. Even if we're not where I want to be, she's still here.

Well, she wasn't for the last four days. But I'm taking a stand now by making the first move toward at least repairing whatever's wrong with our friendship.

She's going through something difficult. Finding out that her ex is starting a family with someone he barely knows after they were together for six years wasn't easy on her. I understand that even if I can't quite relate.

I think I can even understand her tears too. Because, instead of responding to my question, she's started crying. Has she been holding these sobs in this whole time? I ignore the wetness seeping through my T-shirt and hold her closer, allowing her to break down in my arms. I also push us forward, over the threshold of the door, and shut the door behind us. Then I take us over to her couch, where I pick her up, sit down, and cradle her while she quietly cries.

After a few minutes, her shuddering body stills and she sniffles. "Not that well, apparently."

I brush some hair behind her ear. "I'm glad I'm here, then."

"Yeah, me too," she says, gazing at her lap. "I was thinking about going back home, but I couldn't imagine what good that was going to do. I was too confused. So I did"—she shakes her head and takes a big breath—"nothing."

I nod, glad she didn't go back home. Who knows what would have happened? And, if I'm honest, I think she belongs here. With me. But that's selfish, and I can't keep her away from her family.

"Sorry about your shirt."

"Don't worry." I press her head closer to my shoulder. "I was already thinking about burning this one anyway."

She laughs lightly and leans away from me. When our gazes meet, it's like I can't help myself. Like a magnet, I'm drawn right to her lips. Which feel just like I thought they would: soft but full. They're salty from her tears but sweet like maple syrup too. And they move with mine in a slow, unhurried, relaxed pace.

That surprises me. I thought she'd push me away or run off, but she's not. She's still on my lap, still kissing me. She even wraps an arm around my neck and pulls me closer. Then the pace of our kisses speeds up, becomes more frantic, as she pushes me back on the couch and straddles my lap. Above me, she runs her fingers through my shaggy hair and deepens the kiss. My hands go to her waist, gripping her tighter than I probably should.

There's zero way to hide my reaction to this. No way to mask how being this close to her in this way is making me feel. And, if the way she's grinding against me is anything to go by, she feels it and likes it.

Maybe she missed me as much as I missed her.

Or maybe I'm just a replacement for what she's really missing.

Ouch. That thought hits me like a punch to the chest. And completely deflates any and all arousal I felt at how intimately connected we are right now.

When I break the kiss, I pull back and say, "Hey, E. Maybe we should slow down."

Shock shines in her gaze as she looks at me, but she slowly nods and starts to get up. "Sorry. I don't know what came over me." Then she turns her back to me, but I didn't miss the pink in her cheeks and the way she tried to hide her eyes. "I'm gonna go back to bed now."

Before she's too far away from me, I grab her hand and tug on her fingers. When she peeks over her shoulder, I shake my head.

"I'm not leaving after that. I just can't… We can't…" I'd love to find the right words to say without embarrassing the hell out of myself, but nothing's coming out.

"Right. We crossed a line." She nervously tucks some hair behind her ears. "We're just friends. So we shouldn't have done that."

Well, that's not at all what I was going to say. I wanted to tell her that we shouldn't cross that line if that's not what she wants to do. If she's not really in her right mind. If she's only worked up because of what's happening with her ex-boyfriend. I want to do that with her if she wants to do that with me. Because I'm me and not because of any other reason.

But, if that's how she feels...

I clear my throat and swallow hard. "Right," I agree. Because what else am I supposed to say?

"Goodnight, Eli," Erin says quietly. Then she presses her lips into a thin line and walks back to her bedroom.

Leaving me behind and my heart to crash and burn.

Chapter 7
Erin

I guess it's now his turn to ignore me. I've tried calling and texting for the last week. Halfway to his apartment yesterday, I chickened out. Even though I desperately want to see him, if only for a friendly face—but more because he's Eli, my best friend here, the one person in the world I want to be with—I'm embarrassed.

Last Thursday night was humiliating. Sure, he initiated that kiss, but I threw myself at him with no shame whatsoever and was summarily rejected. Because we're friends. Only friends. Friends who shouldn't be kissing. Or doing anything more than innocent hand-holding or sharing a friendly embrace.

How many times have I been reminded of that throughout the last few months? He's either tensed up at or ignored the occasional hand brushes and other times we accidentally touch. At first, I thought it was because we were still just getting to know each other. I assumed something more would lead from it because I've seen the way he looks at me. And his brother and his sister-in-law left no room for argument on the topic, either. Though we adamantly denied it, they too seemed to have been waiting for the inevitable.

Perhaps it's not so inevitable after all.

I threw the "just friends" line out there for him to refute. I had been hoping he'd deny it and finally admit that he cares more for me than he lets on. Yes, I'm a little fragile, given everything I've been through in the last six months. But, as I've been reminded on a few occasions, if a man wants to be with a woman, nothing will stop him from trying to be with her.

So, clearly, *I* need to get the hint. We *are* just friends after all, and I have to wrap my head around that fact. I haven't yet, which is why I'm not that upset about not having seen him since that night.

Today, however, I'm sure I'll run into him. I'm on my way to another protest, and Eli doesn't miss those. I don't want to, either—even if it means seeing him while I'm still feeling mortified. The cause is too important to let that get in the way. So I wait in my car for a few minutes, thinking he'll want a ride. When he doesn't show up, I contemplate calling him, but I don't. If he wanted a ride, he could have asked. And it's not like I haven't tried to get ahold of him, either. So I decide to go.

When I arrive, he's already there, passing out posters to our fellow protesters. I've always admired that he's the one who keeps them and even makes more as our group grows. It's one of the many things I love about him.

Whoa. Wait.

Love?

No. That can't be. For one, it's way too soon. It took me over a year to say that to Derek. Granted, we were super young at the time and I didn't understand what that really meant, but still. We were together for longer than some marriages last, so I can hardly say that I love someone I met a few months ago, right?

Two, we've already established that he doesn't feel that way about me. I don't know what kind of man walks away from the state we were in if he's actually into the woman. Of course, I'm not the authority on how men work, seeing as I've been with only one. But he agreed—we're just friends.

Friends who apparently stare at and admire each other from afar. Well, it's one-sided. I'm the only one doing this. And I won't allow myself to become that creepy stalker who stays friends with someone to get them to love her. So I take my sign and stand as far away from Eli as I can.

Two hours later, as the group starts to trickle away, someone bumps into me. I ignore it—because I'm used to ignoring everything so I don't let the naysayers bring me down—but the person won't allow that. They do it one more time, so I turn around.

And there's Eli. His skin is a little darker than I remember. And the sheen of sweat on his forehead is nothing compared to the damp spots on his shirt. The sun's been beating down on us, so I'm not surprised by that. Though I am surprised by how attractive I find him. This guy stood outside in the blistering heat of early spring to fight for a cause near and dear to my heart. Derek never would have done anything like this with me. So his heartwarming gesture makes him even more endearing.

He cut his hair, too. I didn't notice it from far away, but I see it now. There's no stray lock falling into his eyes. He's not moving it off his face. Yet I have no less of an urge to run my fingers through it. So how in the world am I ever going to get over this so we can go back to being friends?

"Hey, E," he says before collecting a stack of signs from someone leaving the protest. "Thanks for coming out," he tells them and then returns his attention to me and ushers me toward some shade. "Where have you been?"

I gape. "Excuse me? I-I called you, I texted you—"

He laughs a little at me, but not in a mean way. He's amused, and I'll honestly take that over him not being in my life at all. Doesn't mean that it's not infuriating though.

"I even started driving to your place," I continue, "but then—"

"You what?" He's not laughing anymore. No, he's dead serious now. "When was that?"

I hesitantly say, "Yesterday."

"You should have come over," is all he replies with.

"And you should have answered my calls. What happened to the guy who missed his friend after four days?" I hand my sign to him and cross my arms over my chest. "You've been ignoring me for over a week, and after we…" But I can't get the rest of the words out. If I speak about it, I might cry or something.

"That's exactly why I couldn't answer you, E." He looks at the ground as he speaks. "If I did…" Apparently, he can't talk about it, either.

But I don't know why. "What, Eli? I need you to finish your thought this time."

He sighs. "I can't."

I put a hand on my hip. "Why not?" I ask louder than I should have.

All he does is shake his head. He's still not looking at me.

"At least tell me why," I demand. "I deserve to know why you've been ignoring me. It's been over a week, Eli"—I thrust a finger at him as I raise my voice—"and you haven't answered a single text or a call. You haven't emailed me or anything. I think I deserve an—"

"I love you!" he says in a raised voice, finally finding my gaze. Then he closes his eyes, inhales a deep breath, and lets it out through his nose on a rush. In a quieter tone, he finishes with, "That's why."

My hand falls to my side. My mouth falls open. And

my heart falls to my feet. Before it immediately rushes up to my throat and thrashes around. Did he really just say that?

I wait for him to open his eyes. Mostly because I can't speak. But also because I need to see what he really meant by that. We've grown close—as friends—over the last few months. Friendly love is a natural part of that process. Part of me hopes I'm in denial, but part of me believes I need some self-preservation.

"I couldn't answer you because I'd tell you," he clarifies, staring me straight in my wide eyes. "You were clear about how we're just friends, so I went along with it. And then I was the one who needed some time by myself. To let it all go so we could continue to be just friends."

Tears build up in my eyes, but he's not done yet.

"I can't love you, Erin." His shoulders slump forward, and he throws his arms out to his sides, the posters going with them. "I want you in my life, and if that means as just friends, then I have to accept that. And it's probably for the best because you don't live here. You'll probably go back home after graduation. I certainly can't leave my family, and then we may never see each other again."

Well, he has a point there. I still haven't figured that part out even though my parents have been pressuring me to start applying for jobs.

"Plus, you just got out of a serious relationship, and the last thing you need is another guy throwing himself at you right now. And you might randomly decide to take off for some other place where no one knows you. So I haven't wanted to be around you because, when I'm around you, I want to kiss you, and I shouldn't do that again." He wipes sweat off his brow with the short sleeve of his shirt. "I can't do that again," he stresses, shaking his head.

I shake mine too, but for totally different reasons. While he's making a point, I'm straight-up caught off guard. So I start to speak. Nothing comes out, but Eli stops me anyway.

"No, E," he says. "Not if we're just friends."

Chapter 8
Eli

Walking is one of my favorite things. I walked here so I didn't have to torture myself by being in such close proximity to her in her car. And I'd love to walk away from this situation so I don't have to deal with it. Because I just admitted how I feel to Erin. But my brother didn't teach me to walk away.

No, the best things happened to him when he faced them head on. So I'll walk toward this instead. Maybe something good will happen—like perhaps I won't lose her completely.

Or maybe I will. She's staring at me, unable to say anything. Until, a few moments later, words finally make it past her lips.

"You're right." That's all she says on a big exhale. Then she repeats it. "You're right."

I raise an eyebrow at her. "About what?"

She gulps, and her throat bobs with the effort. "Everything." Her curls blow in the light—and very welcome—breeze. "All of it. You're right." She slides her hair over one shoulder to try to tame it, but it's futile. "I did just get out of a relationship. I don't need another one right now. I may decide to up and leave again. And I did tell you that we're just friends. That's all true."

"Okay," I say slowly, stretching the word out. I wasn't expecting or even hoping for that. "So what do we do?"

"We stop being friends, Eli!" she shouts, throwing her arms out to her sides. "Clearly, we can't be friends anymore if you feel that way about me."

Well, then. Maybe nothing good is coming of this after all. And maybe I'll be walking back home now too.

I grit my teeth to fight the twitch in my jaw. "If that's how you feel," I tell her, staring at the sidewalk.

"It is!" she yells. Then she steps closer to me and stabs a finger my way. "Because I can't be friends with you, either!"

I don't know why she's shouting at me, but it seems like she needs to get this out, so I let her. If this is the last contact I'll have with her now that she knows how I feel, I'll take what I can get.

"I lied! I thought that's how you felt—that you wanted to be friends." She thrusts that finger at me again. "That you didn't feel that way about me because you stopped that...that *moment* we had last week. We've had plenty of opportunities to do that in the past, but you've never jumped at the chance. And your family kept making comments about us being together, but you shot them all down. What was I supposed to think?"

A few of the protesters are focusing more on us than they are on holding their signs up for drivers to see. And I'd care, but the woman I love might feel the same way back. So they can stare all they want. Especially when I drop the posters I collected, grip the sides of her face, and kiss her for all of them to see.

I put everything I have into this kiss. We've been holding back for months, depriving ourselves because we thought the other wanted or needed that space. But we've crossed that line now, and I don't ever want to go back.

She does the same, kissing me back with the passion I've always known she's had inside her. She's a fiery free spirit, and I appreciate that about her. If I have my way, I always will. She just has to let me.

So I break our second kiss to say, "But what about—"

"Don't." Her forehead rubs against mine as she shakes her head slightly. "I have answers to all of your questions, and they're good answers. So just kiss me." She smiles, her eyes lighting up as she gazes at me.

Maybe I'm a glutton for punishment, because I do. I give her what she asked for and kiss her. She says she has good answers for all of my worries, and I don't know how to trust that completely, but it'll do for now.

Well, only for a second. Then I have to say, "No, seriously."

She laughs, but it has a frustrated edge to it. "Come on, E."

"I know." I chuckle too. "But I promise not to … what did you say? Stop our moment? I won't do that again if you answer a few questions," I say, holding two fingers up in a "Scout's honor" way.

As she wraps her arms around my waist, she huffs out a breath. "Fine. Two." Then she grins up at me.

"Okay. One." I grip her hips and hold her at a distance so I'm not tempted to forget my questions and go back to kissing her. "What are your plans for after graduation?"

After a deep inhale, she says, "I have no idea, but I do think Arizona will have more opportunities for me than Indiana will."

That's a relief. And it sounds nice, but… "What if you decide to move again?" I ask her. "I can't leave like you can."

She glances at the sky. "I get that concern too." Then she looks me in the eye and drags her fingers down my arms. "But I left home because everything there was a mess. Literally everything. No one but Roxie understood me, and she didn't even agree with me, so I set out to find something new."

That also sounds nice, but… "Do you think you found it?" I gulp, nerves tingling in my stomach as I await her answer.

She rubs my nose with hers. "What I think is…"

I pull her closer to me as she tortures me by making me wait. "Woman. You're gonna kill me."

Her giggles hit me right in my heart, where I hope she'll stay forever. "I think I found my something new."

My heart takes off at a sprint. But if I've learned anything since I met Erin, it's that I need her to say exactly what she's really feeling. The whole truth.

"And what's that something new, E? Be honest with me," I tell her.

"It's not this Arizona heat," she says around a laugh, fanning herself a little.

I drop my arms from her hips. "I swear to god—"

But she kisses me again before I can finish my frustrated sentence. "You, E. You're my something new. You, your family…" Her eyes shine with happy tears. "Everything about you. We see eye to eye on some really important stuff," she says, gesturing to the posters at our feet. Then she smiles at me. "So I think you're my something new."

"Thank goodness!" With my arms around her back, I press her to me. "We'll take it one day at a time, E. You just promise to tell me what you need from me. Please."

She nods and rests her chin on my shoulder. "I promise."

"Good." I kiss her hair. "For now, though, someone needs to help me clean up the posters I've dropped twice because of you." Leaning away, I wink at her.

Laughing, she swats at my chest. "Well, while I'm still here, I guess I can do that." She bends forward and winks back at me.

Oh, this woman will keep me on my toes for sure. But I can't ask for anything more than that.

Except for maybe her—for the rest of my life.

Eliza Boyd is a contemporary women's fiction, romance, and short story author. When she's not reading, writing, or working, she can be found walking around her neighborhood (for exercise, not for stalking), eating delicious vegan food, taking photos of her pets, or binge-watching something on Netflix with her husband. Learn more at elizaboydwrites.com

THE SMUGGLERS LEGION
KATHERINE BOGLE

The small shack Rikkard called home lay at the end of the sand-strewn street. Heat rose from the sand dunes in waves, blurring the horizon. If it weren't for his steel-toed boots, his feet would have already melted to the asphalt, rendering him a permanent fixture of the Old Boston Outskirts.

His muscles ached from a long day at the booster factory. He might not mind if it weren't for what always awaited him at home.

Rikkard sighed as he reached the end of the lane. Planks of rotten wood fell away from the small front porch, poorly concealing the gaping hole in the second step. At least the steel-plated door he'd installed last year was still intact. The same couldn't be said for the rest of the decaying house.

His boots thudded against the three steps bringing him to the porch. The wood groaned beneath him.

Christ.

He shook his head, long strands of black hair tickling his ears. His heart hammered faster as he pulled his keys from his pocket. They jingled softly.

Maybe he should have picked up an extra shift. Maybe he could have stopped by Jules Tavern for a while and watched the news on the holoscreen. Anything to keep him from coming home.

He took a deep breath. There was no point in backing out now.

Rikkard turned the key and pushed the door open. It swung inward, and he stepped inside. The heavy scent of mold and body odor assaulted his nose. His nostrils flared as he closed the door behind him.

"Rikky?" the soft voice of his mother drifted from the living room just outside the small kitchen he'd stepped into.

He froze, his fingers glued to the doorknob. He should have taken an extra shift.

"Rikky!" she slurred out the nickname he hated.

"Hi, mom." He dragged himself away from the door and into the kitchen.

Grime dirtied broken tiles, and cabinet doors hung free of their hinges. Rikkard yanked a chipped coffee mug with the smudged logo of something called the Boston Red Sox from a cabinet.

The fridge's contents shook, clanging against one another as he pulled open the door. The blue-tinged plastic water jug was empty.

He worked his jaw as he slammed the door shut.

"Rikky, you're making a racket." The couch springs squeaked as she shifted.

"Have you even gotten off the couch today, mom?"

"What? I-I... Don't take that tone with your mother."

He could hardly understand her words over her stammering. Rikkard rolled his eyes and crossed his arms as he waited in the doorway of the living room. His shoulder pressed against the doorframe, forcing the wood to creak in annoyance.

"I'm waiting." He already knew the answer. After his

father died eight years ago in a bar brawl he'd been the sole provider for his mother's booster addiction.

Though the alien government, the Aldar Dominion, only sanctioned the use of the drug enhancements they called boosters in "safe zones", it wasn't difficult to find them on the black market.

"Rikkard Aven Gunnar." Gabrielle sat up in a mess of blankets and limbs. Two fans stood on either side of the sofa, blowing her wild black hair from her shoulders. It stuck in all directions, greasy from lack of care. "Do not speak to your mother like that." She worked her jaw as if testing out her words. Her half-lidded gaze, bloodshot eyes and pale lips told him all he needed to know.

She was higher than the cruise ships flying overhead.

His fists clenched and he bit back a growl of frustration. Every damn time. Every damn day. This is what she did. She used the money he made to get high and forget their shitty life in the Outskirts.

As if he didn't want to forget it all too, but someone had to keep them alive.

Rikkard spun on his heels and stomped back toward the door.

"Rikky, where are y-you going?"

He slammed the door behind him and leapt down the steps onto the sand-covered walkway. He needed to get out of this house. This place. This town.

He was so tired of this. Tired of taking care of his drug-addicted mother. Tired of being the adult when he'd just turned nineteen. Tired of being stuck in this small town with nothing but gangbangers, pirates, and drug addicts like Gabrielle.

Rikkard shook his head as he trudged down Main Street back the way he'd come. He needed a drink. He couldn't deal with his mother while sober.

The faux-leather stool at Jules' Tavern squeaked beneath

him as he sat. Rikkard grimaced and wrinkled his nose as he adjusted. The stench of spoiled beer was nearly overpowering, reaching up his nostrils and taking hold. He'd have a hell of a time getting the smell out of his clothes.

"What can I get you?" Jules, the old broad who owned the tavern, leaned against the bar, a rag in one hand and a flirty smile on her face. Her lips twisted as she batted her false eyelashes at him.

Rikkard bit back a sigh. "Whiskey."

"You got it, handsome." Jules winked and spun back toward the display of aged liquor bottles lining the back wall. Though most of them had been emptied long ago and filled with whatever new crap the locals had concocted, Jules sometimes splurged and poured him a drink from her secret stash in the cabinet below the display.

She reached for a dingy brown bottle on the shelf. Sadly, today was not one of those days.

Shouts rose from the booths lining the back of the bar. Rikkard glanced over his shoulder. The local gang howled with laughter as one of them slammed the fist of the other against the table. The bottles rattled as the man stood, flexing his biceps; he'd won the arm wrestle.

"You look tired, Rik. Anything you want to talk about?" Jules set a half-full glass of whiskey in front of him. Her blond curls, too blond to be real, bobbed around her chubby cheeks as she reached for a rag and went about cleaning an empty glass.

"No thanks, Jules." He plucked the glass from the table and swallowed back a large mouthful. Whiskey burned his throat, all the way to his stomach. He slammed the glass back down.

"All right, sweetie." Jules nodded and slid off to attend the other patrons.

Rikkard spun the glass in hand, trying to calm the burning irritation rising in his chest. Shouts from the gang members echoed in his ears as he rubbed his fingers over week-old scruff. Now he remembered why he didn't stop at the tavern earlier: the constant noise and stench drove him mad.

He swallowed back the rest of the whiskey. Though the tavern was mostly one long room, it was usually quieter in the back where the holoscreen played the evening news.

"Jules." He tapped the bar beside his glass.

Jules returned in a flash, filling up his glass before returning the bottle back to the shelf.

"Thanks." He slipped from the stool.

"No problem, doll."

Rikkard slid around drunks hunched at the bar and stepped over those already passed out on the floor. Jules let the frequent customers be as long as they kept coming back and kept buying.

Another chorus of laughter and fists slamming against tables sent the dish lights overhead swinging, throwing shadows across Rikkard's blue eyes as he skirted an empty pool table.

At the back of the bar, the dim light fell to long shadows in every corner. With no lights overhead, only the glow of the holoscreen propped against the wall feebly lit the few regulars huddled on stools.

An alien newscaster occupied the screen, bright blue skin and dark eyes paired with protruding cheekbones and a narrow chin. The man yammered on about the recently elected Governor of New Manhattan as the few patrons sitting around the screen yawned.

Rikkard found a quiet spot in a row of narrow booths with only two others occupied. He slouched onto the faux-leather, ignoring the quiet whispers of the men behind him. People either came to Jules' Tavern to drink until they passed out, or to carry out some sort of shady deal.

He swallowed more whiskey. It burned his throat and seared his tastebuds. He shook his head. Though he wasn't a fan of liquor in general, it did help calm his irritation and numb the general unpleasantness of the Outskirts. If there was no leaving the awful place, at least he had something to make it somewhat bearable.

"Smugglers are bringing another shipment of boosters in tonight," one of the men behind him mumbled. His words slurred. Drunk, of course.

"'Aye, what kind this time?" another asked. Maybe a bit soberer.

"No clue, but they're asking a lot of questions about the factory."

Rikkard froze. The booster factory?

"Why?"

"A new prototype they're interested in, I bet."

"A prototype, eh? What do you 'spose they'd pay for such a thing?"

Those who weren't getting high every day spent most of their days working in the booster factory. Though most of it had once been automated, the Aldar Dominion stripped half the machinery from the factory in an effort to 'bring jobs back to the Outskirts'.

"A thousand credits at least."

A thousand credits? His heart raced. What could he do with that kind of money? Get out of the Outskirts. Get a new job – a new life. He could buy an actual speeder with that kind of money – not the junkyard speeders they sold in town.

"Ain't no way to get into the research lab, though." The man sighed. "If there were, I'd be rich by now." He chuckled.

Rikkard spun in his seat and stood. "Where can I find these people?" He leaned against the booth.

The first man to speak had a jagged scar through his eyebrow and a shaven head. He arched an eyebrow. "Listening in on our conversation, eh, boy?"

"Where can I find them?" Rikkard narrowed his eyes.

The men exchanged a look. They grinned before bursting into laughter.

The second man slammed his palm against the table and held his gut. "You'd be crazy to mess with the Smugglers Legion, you stupid boy!"

Rikkard ground his teeth together and grabbed the man by his collar, yanking him out of the booth. The man yelped as Rikkard threw him to the floor. "Where?"

The man went bug-eyed, staring up at Rikkard as he stammered out something unintelligible.

The first man leapt to his feet. "You're fucking crazy, kid!"

Rikkard levelled him a cold glare.

"Go to Radley's in Bakura. Talk to the bartender," the man buckled. He swayed as if he might fall. If these two hadn't been so drunk they might have tried to fight Rikkard. It was sheer dumb luck they were too wasted to stand.

Rikkard nodded. He stepped away from the men and grabbed his glass. He took another sip of his drink, ignoring the sharp bite of liquor as he slammed the glass back down and left the bar.

The old navy ship turned black market rose atop the sand, a black mass on the horizon. Rikkard had never seen Bakura, but he'd heard plenty of stories. The worst of the worst occupied it. Everything from gambling, to illegal liquor trade, slave exchange and gun smuggling took place in Bakura.

He gulped. He'd never been beyond the Outskirts, never been further than the Old Boston Ruins. Going to Bakura took him away from everything he'd ever known. His heart raced with anticipation.

After purchasing an old broken down speeder with what little savings he had, Rikkard had taken a small bag, said goodbye to his unconscious mother, and left. He was done with the Outskirts. Done with all of it. His mother would survive on her own. She had enough connections, 'friends' and drug dealers to keep her going.

If he could make this happen, if he could get this prototype to the Smugglers Legion, maybe he'd be able to start over. Maybe he'd find a new purpose, a new direction. If he could save enough, maybe one day he'd be able to afford cloning. Maybe one day he'd join the immortal clones of Earth.

The rumble of his one-seat scrap speeder slowed as he landed on the wide deck next to a row of much nicer cruisers. Tall and wide, with a hood and front view port instead of open to the wind like his. Some were sleek and curved – alien. Others were made of scrap metal like his and dirtied with sand.

Rikkard pulled the goggles from his face, leaving them to dangle around his neck. A large vault-like door stood ajar – a definite upgrade from the dilapidated navy ship. Two men in black leather with gun holsters strapped to their hips and assault rifles slung over their shoulders, smoked cigarettes next to a metal cruiser. Their dark eyes darted in his direction for only a heartbeat.

At least his rugged appearance came in handy somewhere.

Rikkard cleared his throat and pulled the keys from his speeder. He still couldn't believe a speeder that used keys existed in the twenty-fourth century, but it was all he could afford.

He dismounted the speeder, and swung his small brown backpack over his shoulder, passed by the two gun-toting men, and entered Bakura.

The clang of metal, whizz of a saw and general rowdy chatter he associated with a bar, rang through the hollow metal space. Whatever the room had once been, it was no longer.

Rows and rows of metal stands and shelves occupied the floor a story below. Dozens upon dozens of men and women milled by, most decorated like old war heroes:

metal or leather armor slung across their chest, and guns strapped to every limb.

Rikkard quirked a brow. Had he known wearing weapons in the open was acceptable, he wouldn't have hidden his old revolver in the bottom of his bag.

A metal grate walkway curved above the market, leading toward every end of the ship.

Rikkard glanced back and forth, rooted to the spot. No bar in sight. Gunslingers, slavers, and drug dealers – sure, but no bar.

"Hm." His mouth twitched in irritation.

If the men at Jules Tavern lied to him, they'd never see the inside of that bar again – if they saw anything again at all.

Following the walkway, Rikkard made his way to the back end of the ship. If the market occupied the front, maybe bars and other services occupied the back.

He stepped off the metal grates and into a long hall. The chatter of the market faded, replaced with the creaking of the ship. Dim lights inside metal dishes flickered overhead, strung up with some sort of wiring that dangled a few inches from the ceiling.

Had he been a few inches taller, his head would brush the lights.

Gentle footsteps echoed in the hallway, but no one treaded down the dingy hall. Where then? He glanced over his shoulder. Nothing but shadows.

The footsteps moved in time with his. Could it just be a coincidence?

He picked up the pace, lengthening his stride.

The footsteps moved in time with his. So it wasn't by chance; someone was following him.

His heart raced faster than his feet. He needed to get the gun from his bag, but he couldn't do that faster than someone could draw theirs. He cursed himself for leaving it at the bottom, buried beneath clothes and bottled water – all which would be useless if he died at the hands of some lowlife.

Rikkard gritted his teeth. He would not go down like this.

He spun, yanking his backpack from over his shoulder and slinging it onto his chest.

Wide blue eyes stared up at him. Rikkard grabbed the wrist of the pickpocket's outstretched hand, and twisted her arm behind her back.

"Let go of me!" she cried.

Rikkard took a deep breath to calm his racing heart. Just a girl, no more than fifteen or sixteen. What the hell was she doing in Bakura?

"Trying to steal from me?" His grip on her wrist tightened.

She hissed out a breath. "No! I was just... I was just following you! I haven't seen you around here before."

He raised an eyebrow. He didn't believe her for a second. "Why are you here?"

It was her turn to raise an eyebrow. "Why am I here? I live here."

People lived in Bakura?

Rikkard glanced at the grungy floors and walls, the flickering lights, and back towards the black market. He couldn't imagine why anyone would live in such a horrible place.

"Why?" he asked.

She scoffed and rolled her eyes. "Where the hell else am I supposed to go?"

Rikkard worked his jaw back and forth. Maybe living in the Outskirts wasn't so bad. Not compared to this place.

He released her, stepping away and returning his backpack to his shoulder.

The pickpocket spun around, her short brown curls bouncing around her face. "You're letting me go?"

He nodded.

She turned to make a run for it.

"Wait." He reached out. She glanced back. "Where can

I find Radley's?"

She nodded in the direction he'd been heading. "Not far that way. You can't miss it."

"Thanks." Rikkard turned. "Be careful."

She chuckled. "You too, newbie." Her footsteps retreated the way he'd come.

Rikkard heaved a sigh. He didn't have time to dwell on the happenings of Bakura. He had places to be.

Trudging down the long grim hall, Rikkard sifted through his backpack until he pulled his revolver from the bottom. Once it was out, he swung his backpack back over his shoulder and stuck the gun into the back of his pants, securing it with his belt. The cold metal sent a shiver up his spine.

He hoped he wouldn't need to use it. It had been years since he'd shot a gun.

The bar-chatter increased in volume until a neon sign broke the bleakness of the hall. 'Radley's Bar', it said. Finally, he was at the right place.

Rikkard took a deep breath before stepping inside.

Music blared from an old jukebox at the back of the bar. He'd only ever seen one like it before, years ago in Jules' Tavern. It had long since broken from lack of maintenance. The stench of vomit, alcohol and body odor stung his nostrils and soured his stomach. Nasty.

The same gun-toting, knife-wielding, scar infested sort occupied the tables on the right side of the bar, as well as the dark booths at the back, and a few of the stools at the long, metal bar winding around the left end of the room. The patrons didn't glance up, immersed in whatever banter or games they played to amuse themselves.

The bartender poured clear liquid from a blue bottle into a filthy glass. He glanced up, his eyes ultraviolet in color. Rikkard clenched his fists to keep from starting in surprise. The bartender was a clone. He hadn't met many in his life, but the smooth skin and artificial eye color were unmistakable.

Rikkard swallowed the lump in his throat and approached the bar, eyeing a torn suede stool at the end, far away from the other patrons. He didn't want the whole place overhearing his request; he didn't need competition for this booster prototype.

Slipping onto the seat, he glanced at the rest of the men sitting at the bar stools. Most were slouched, faces drawn and skin graying. He knew the look of alcoholics well, and these were no different than the ones in Jules' Tavern.

"What can I get you?" The bartender locked eyes with him. His pupils narrowed as he assessed Rikkard.

"Information." Rikkard didn't miss a beat.

The black-skinned man's lips quirked to one side in a sly smile. "Of course." He moved to step away.

"The Smugglers Legion," Rikkard said before the bartender could take a second step. The man froze. Rikkard had his attention. "Where can I find them?"

The violet gaze of the bartender returned. "You want to mess with the Smugglers?" His lips spread in a toothy grin.

"I just want to know where I can find them." His fist clenched on the smooth counter top. He needed this information. Without it, he had nowhere to go but home, and that was the last thing he wanted.

The bartender sized him up before nodding. "The booth at the back." He motioned toward the darkest corner of the bar. "Eria should be there."

Rikkard nodded, unable to hide his relieved sigh as he stood. "Thanks."

The man chuckled. "Don't thank me."

Rikkard glanced back as the bartender returned to the other patrons, shaking his head in disbelief. What was he getting himself into?

It was too late to back out now.

Steeling himself, Rikkard nearly jogged across the bar to keep himself from backing out. If he wanted to stay out of the Outskirts permanently, he had to do this. He had to do something to get out of there.

"Are you Eria?" Rikkard hovered beside the booth.

Two figures sat in the shadows. One remained cloaked, a hood drawn over their head. The other narrowed large, nearly bug-eyed, navy blue eyes at him – an alien.

"What do you want?" the alien growled and stuck out his narrow chin.

Rikkard glared. "I'm here to speak with the Smugglers Legion."

The twisted frown of the alien quirked in amusement. "Are you now?"

"Yes." Rikkard gritted his teeth as he glanced between them. With the lights so weak, it was hard to make out the expression of the second, but if Eria was the one in charge, that was who he needed to speak with – not whatever lackey this was.

"You must be new here," the man continued. "If the Smugglers are interested, they'll contact you."

Rikkard snapped his lips shut to hold back his growl of irritation. "Look, I'm not here to speak to you. I'm here to speak with Eria, or whoever runs the Smugglers."

The man stood quickly, banging his hips against the table in the process. He narrowed his eyes at Rikkard. "No one speaks with the Captain unless spoken to."

"Kayl." The soft voice of a woman stopped him. The cloaked figure held up slender fingers covered in golden rings. "That's enough."

Kayl twisted his wide jaw back and forth, mumbled a foreign curse Rikkard couldn't make out, and took a seat.

The woman flicked her hood back to reveal long black waves tied back from her face. Twisting black tattoos wrapped her neck and part of her cheekbone. Her cheeks dimpled as her thick lips twisted in an amused smile. Her poreless skin marked her as a clone.

"Captain Eria." She offered her hand.

Rikkard glanced at Eria's bodyguard, or whatever he was, before taking her hand firmly. Eria squeezed and shook his hand before releasing it.

"Why don't you take a seat?" She motioned to where Kayl sat.

Kayl worked his jaw before he slid out of the booth. He stood next to Eria, leaning against the wooden edge as Rikkard slid onto the faux-leather.

"What's your name?" Eria's gaze trailed from his hair to his chest.

"Rikkard," he said.

"Rikkard," she purred his name. "What have you come to see me for?" She raised a tattooed eyebrow, her cat-like eyes continuing their inspection under thick lashes.

He'd never seen a woman like this before. Sure, there were plenty in the Outskirts, but most were drug addicts like his mother, with sunken cheeks, graying skin and vacant eyes. None were as alive, or as vibrant as this woman.

"I've been told you're looking for a booster prototype." Rikkard tapped his fingers against the table, unable to hold back his anxiousness.

"I see the word has gotten out." Eria exchanged a look with Kayl. "And you think you can get this prototype?"

Rikkard nodded. "I work at the factory outside the Old Boston Ruins. The research lab is always coming up with new prototypes."

Her dark eyes sparked with interest. "So you heard about this... opportunity, at Jules' Tavern, I suspect?"

He stiffened. "Yes."

"Excellent." She glanced at Kayl. "You've done well."

Kayl nodded and crossed his arms over his chest. Tattoos swirled erratically around his exposed biceps and forearms. Rikkard had heard once that the alien tattoos portrayed the emotions of their host. What was Kayl feeling?

"What do you want in exchange for the prototype?" Eria placed her fingers on her cheek, long black nails tapping against her temple.

His heart pounded against his ribs. This was it. He was going to be free of the Outskirts. He would be free of everything that caged him. "A job."

Eria raised both eyebrows. "A job?" She laughed. "You want to work for the Smugglers Legion full-time?" He nodded. "Well, well. You're a fine one, indeed." Eria reached across the table, trailing the tip of her nail across the back of his hand.

Rikkard froze.

"If you can get the prototype in lab four, you can have a job on my personal team."

"Captain!" Kayl gasped.

Eria held up a hand. Kayl's lips snapped shut. "What say you?"

"It's a deal." His heart hammered faster.

"There is one condition, my dear." Eria retracted her fingers and smiled. "I want you to take Kayl with you."

Kayl stilled but didn't say a word.

Rikkard's jaw tightened. It would be difficult enough getting himself inside the lab at the factory. Having an extra to tow around wouldn't shift the odds in his favor.

"Bring Kayl, or there's no deal, Rikkard." Her smile fell.

He sighed inwardly. "Fine."

Something devious flickered through her gaze. "Excellent. Then it's a deal."

Rikkard and Kayl stood atop a hill overlooking a large brick building with smokestacks no longer in use. The old factory had somehow remained standing after solar flares ravaged the earth three hundred years ago. With a parking lot covered in sand and a few speeders remaining on the dark lot, it shouldn't be too difficult to gain access to the factory. Or so Rikkard hoped.

He bit the inside of his cheek. If he failed this mission, he'd be stuck in the Outskirts for Aldar knew how long.

What was worse, if they were caught, he would end up in prison for the rest of his days.

He shook his head. He couldn't think about that now.

"This is it?" Kayl blinked his second set of eyelids at him.

Rikkard glanced at the alien. "Yes."

"What's your plan?"

There wasn't one, not really. But he couldn't say that. Rikkard worked his jaw. "We'll go in the employee entrance, across the work floor to the elevator. Research is on the third floor. Once we're up there, we can find lab four." Or so he hoped. In reality, Rikkard had never gotten off the first floor. He had never been to the research wing, or even ventured near the elevator.

What was security like on the third floor? How would they get past it?

Though hardly anyone but the researchers worked this late at night, there was still plenty to get them in trouble.

Kayl raised the skin on his forehead where a human eyebrow would be as if asking is that it?

Rikkard shrugged, and Kayl sighed.

"Fine. What gear are you running?" Kayl pulled a sleek metallic black laser pistol from his hip. He switched the safety off and it whined while charging.

Rikkard pulled the old metal revolver from the back of his pants.

Kayl scoffed. "Seriously?" He rolled his eyes. "Take this." Kayl yanked a second laser gun from its holster on his other hip and handed it to Rikkard.

Both of Rikkard's brows rose as he inspected the sleek shape, wide barrel and thick grip. It wasn't nearly as heavy as the revolver. It was lighter than most dishware.

"Thanks." Rikkard returned his revolver to his backpack.

He twisted the laser pistol in his hands. He'd never used his gun on a person before, just cans on a fence during target practice with his dad nearly eight years ago.

Since then he'd practiced, but never used it in an actual firefight. He'd always been careful to stay away from situations where a gun might be needed. What if he was forced to participate in a shoot out? What if he needed to kill someone to save his own skin? His fingers tightened on the grip. What lengths would he go to, to secure his freedom?

Cold settled in his gut.

"Don't mention it." Kayl fiddled with his belt, pulling open pouches and producing two black disks no larger than his thumbnail. "Put this on."

"What is it?" Rikkard turned the small piece of plastic over in his hand. Ridges marked one side, while the other was smooth.

"A mask." Kayl pressed the plastic dot to his cheek. Black mesh burst from within, enveloping his entire jaw, nose and mouth.

Rikkard hadn't even thought of wearing a mask. He held it to his stubbly cheek and pressed his finger against the indent. Fabric burst free and wrapped his jaw. Somehow he could still breathe easily.

"Ready?" Kayl asked.

Rikkard took a deep breath. "Ready."

"Lead the way."

Rikkard nodded and began the slow descent to the parking lot below. Sand dipped beneath him, and slid down the steep hill as they eased their way across the slope. Two floodlights lit the parking lot, but the employee entrance nestled next to a large dumpster was much more shadowed.

If they skirted the parking lot, they could stay clear of the security cameras. Though Rikkard was only aware of a few, he'd prefer to make their entrance as quiet as possible.

They raced around the parking lot, but slowed as they rounded the corner of the building by the employee entrance.

He froze.

A man leaned against the dumpster, a cigarette burning between his lips. Smoke filled the air as he exhaled. Rikkard didn't recognize him. The man must have been from the nightshift.

Kayl nudged his elbow.

This gave Rikkard an idea. While he'd planned to use his own keycard, if they used this man's, the break-in could never be traced back to Rikkard. He smirked beneath his mask.

Rikkard motioned for Kayl to round one side of the dumpster while he went around the front. After a long moment, Kayl nodded in agreement and disappeared into the shadows.

His heart raced and his palms sweat as he rounded the edge of the dumpster.

The man arched an eyebrow, and stepped back toward the entrance, ready to flee. "Hey, who are you? What are you doing here?" His words slurred as if he'd been drinking. Rikkard wouldn't be surprised if he had. The factory work wasn't exactly brain surgery.

While the man was distracted by Rikkard, Kayl swung around the backside of the dumpster and slammed his elbow into the man's skull.

He toppled to the ground in a heap, his still lit cigarette bouncing across the sand.

Rikkard bent down and plucked the keycard dangling on a clip from the front of the unconscious worker's jean jacket. He straightened and flashed the keycard at Kayl. Understanding lit Kayl's wide alien eyes.

Satisfaction at having surprised the man warmed his stomach as he leapt up the stairs to the thick metal door. Rikkard swiped the card over a wide silver keypad. It dinged, and the door unlocked. Wind brushed his cheeks like a seal being undone.

Inside the factory, the constant whir and clang of metal reverberated through the air. Three-story high machinery moved in every direction, twisting like steel monsters. Kayl looked up, inspecting the machines, while Rikkard led the way.

Under an overhang, shadows reigned, bathing them in darkness and allowing safe passage until they reached the main floor. A long walkway spread between the rows of machines. The few night-shift workers occupied several of the lifts, but they didn't so much as spare the intruders a glance.

The cement floor led to a sleek metal elevator with a glass shaft above it. It lead up to the third floor where a row of glass windows let the researchers observe the lower workings from above.

The elevator never quite fit in with the rest of the factory. Whereas the rest of the building was old, the machinery rusting and constantly jamming, the elevator was brand new – alien, much like the distant cities they'd created. Though Rikkard had never travelled to one of the cities, he'd heard stories and seen pictures on the holoscreen at Jules'. The buildings were huge; some stretching two hundred stories tall with sleek, white, metal or glass panels all the way down each side. They were unbelievable, much like a glass elevator sitting in the middle of a brick factory.

"What now?" Kayl whispered.

Rikkard halted. He'd nearly forgotten Kayl was there. "Dead ahead." He stepped out of the safety of shadows. Instead of sprinting across the open space, he walked casually, glancing at the workers on duty. Not a single pair of eyes flitted in their direction, though a few did take long chugs from their flasks. No wonder it had been so easy to catch the man outside off guard; they were all drunk.

They reached the elevator and Rikkard swiped the keycard across the panel. Instead of dinging, it clanked, red flashing across the silver screen. Damn.

No clearance.

"Shit." Rikkard tried again, only to get the same result.

Kayl sighed. "Step aside." He shoved Rikkard with his

shoulder.

Rikkard stumbled back, heat seeping into his chest. He glowered at Kayl.

The alien pried the panel from the wall and pulled a thin piece of plastic from his tool belt.

"What are you doing?" Rikkard asked.

Kayl hardly glanced his way. He opened a tiny hatch at the bottom of the device and yanked a thin cord from within, attaching it to a port inside the panel. Rikkard shut his mouth against any more complaints. Whatever Kayl was doing, it was more than he could.

The plastic illuminated like a phone screen, glowing for a moment before turning black. Green type flashed across the screen in waves. Kayl typed something onto the surface, and the once red panel flashed green.

The elevator doors chimed open.

Kayl pulled the cord free of the panel and returned the phone-like device to his belt. "What are you waiting for?" He stepped inside the elevator.

Rikkard shook his head and joined him. Now he saw why Eria had sent Kayl along. Rikkard wasn't half as prepared for this mission as he should have been.

The elevator lurched upward; sailing smoothly past the monstrous machines to the third floor where a row of black-clad guards waited by the elevator door.

"Shit," they both said in unison.

"Get down!" Kayl leapt to the side of the elevator doors, as did Rikkard.

He pinned himself to the wall as the doors opened and laser fire hit the back of the elevator, burning the glass, but not piercing it.

Rikkard gritted his teeth. This is exactly what he'd been afraid of – a shoot out. He pulled his new laser pistol from the waist of his pants. Cold dread sat in his gut. If he couldn't get out of this, he'd die, or worse, be trapped in an alien prison from the rest of his life. He wasn't ready for either of those outcomes, but he couldn't see a way out of this either.

"On my mark!" Kayl snapped.

Rikkard looked at the man.

Kayl motioned for him to crouch down. Rikkard obeyed. The alien held his hands to his ears for a brief moment. Rikkard mimicked him. Kayl nodded and produced a small silver ball from his utility belt. He pressed a button on its surface. A red light flashed as he tossed it out into the hall before covering his ears, mouthing: three, two, one.

An explosion rocked the entire factory. Smoke filled the corridor, and chunks of cement and brick fell from the walls. Glass walls shattered, spreading shards in every direction. Dust fell from the ceiling in the hall, coating the bloody remains of the security guards strewn across the once pristine white floor.

Rikkard's eyes widened as he stared at severed limbs, and ragged torsos. His ears rang, even with the explosion long over.

He'd seen dead bodies before. Lots of them. But most of them were covered in vomit and sand – not their own charred, gory remains.

Kayl grabbed Rikkard by the arm, yanked him up and shoved him into the hall. Rikkard stumbled, barely getting his feet under him before he crashed to the floor. Kayl led the way, leaping over carcasses, severed limbs and rubble with relative ease.

Rikkard followed, unable to do anything else.

They'd just killed twelve people. There was no dodging penalty for a crime as heinous as this. Surely, they'd be sent to jail, or a work camp of some kind. There was no better fate for murderers.

But what if they didn't get caught? What if they got the prototype and survived this? He swallowed his doubt and squinted through the dust stinging his eyes.

Metal numbers flashed across the glass-walled rooms on either side of them. Only the walls by the elevator had been decimated.

The third floor was so different from the rest of the factory; it was hard to believe they were still in the same building.

A dark-haired man in a lab coat leapt from a room, eyes wild and glazed with fear.

"Grab him!" Kayl shouted.

Rikkard lurched forward. One of the researchers. If they could get his keycard, they'd have access to the entire floor. They'd get the prototype and get out of here, before local law enforcers arrived.

"No!" the man yelped as Rikkard took one arm and Kayl grabbed the other. They wrenched his arms behind his back, forcing him to cry out once more.

"Your keycard!" Kayl barked.

"M-My k-keycard?" he sputtered.

"Where is it?" Rikkard's heart pounded in his ears as he patted the man down until he found a plastic sleeve with an ID card inside. "Got it."

"Where is lab four?" Kayl glanced at the numbers around them. There didn't seem to be a pattern or order to them, not that they could see through the dust anyway.

"Please don't hurt me," the man whined.

Kayl rolled his eyes and twisted the man's arm. "Help us, and we won't." The man winced.

"That way!" The researcher nodded at the far end of the hall.

Kayl glanced at Rikkard and motioned down the hall.

Rikkard released the man, making sure Kayl had a hold of him before he raced the length of the corridor.

4.

Finally.

Rikkard waved for Kayl to follow. Once Kayl was on his way, Rikkard swiped the keycard over the panel beside the door. His heart pounded ferociously. This was it. They were almost there. Once they had the prototype, they'd escape on their speeders and head back to Bakura. Then, he'd be free. Free of the Outskirts. Free of his mom. Free of the old Rikkard Gunnar.

He stepped inside as Kayl joined him.

Counters lined the walls, clear cabinets hovering above them. Several long, metal tables stretched across the middle of the room with small, silver disks similar to, but larger than, holosceens placed on top of them. Long strings of numbers flashed across the screens. He swiped a hand through it. It didn't flicker like a holoscreen would.

"Where's the prototype they're working on in this lab?" Kayl slammed the squirming researcher onto a silver stool. He crossed his arms over his chest. The researcher didn't dare try to run.

"I-I d-don't know," the man stammered and glanced around.

Rikkard flipped through files spread across the tables, and searched cabinets full of medical instruments and vials of every color. He had no idea what any of it was.

"You work here, of course you know." Kayl grabbed him by the throat.

The researcher jabbed a fist into Kayl's gut, making him double over and cry out. Their captive leapt for the door, his eyes widened with adrenaline and terror.

Rikkard slid across the metal counter and grabbed the man's shoulder, wrenching him backward. The researcher spun and stumbled, grabbing onto the first thing his fingers found: Rikkard's mask. It ripped from his face, the fabric retracting into the disk as it fell to the floor.

Rikkard growled. Heat burned through his chest as his fist crashed into the researcher's jaw.

The man fell to the floor in a heap. Rikkard kicked him onto his back. "Just tell us where it is!"

Blood poured from the man's busted lip. The researcher stammered incoherently.

The whine of a laser pistol stopped the man's

mumbling. Rikkard glanced at Kayl who flicked the safety off his gun and held it to the researcher's forehead.

"Tell us where the prototype is, or die." His voice lowered, deep and menacing. "It's your choice."

"The vault at the back! Beneath the counter!" the researcher blurted. Rikkard hardly understood what he uttered over the stuttering, but Kayl must have.

He flew across the lab and ripped open a cabinet door. A silver safe with a fingerprint panel on one side, barred their way to the prototype. Rikkard tugged the researcher to his feet, across the lab and dumped him in front of the safe.

"Open it," Rikkard commanded.

"They'll kill me!" the researcher wailed.

Kayl rolled his eyes and prodded the man with his gun. "Do it."

The researcher shook his head as he reached out, but hesitated with his thumb over the panel. Rikkard grabbed his wrist and thrust his hand down.

Green lit the exterior of the panel and the safe clicked open. As soon as Kayl swung the door open, Rikkard threw the researcher back. The man cowered against the cabinets, pulling his knees up to his chest.

"Is it there?" His heart beat against his ribcage. Rikkard could taste freedom. He'd never been this close.

Kayl grinned. "It's here." He pulled a small case from the inside: ribbed metal with frosted glass windows in each side.

They stepped away from the safe. Kayl set the metal case on the table beside them and flicked open the clasps on the top like a briefcase. Nestled inside black fabric was a bag of bright green capsules.

"Is this it? Rikkard asked. It had to be.

Kayl nodded and re-sealed the case. "It is."

"Let's get back." Rikkard was careful not to say Bakura. He was sure the researcher would be questioned about them thoroughly.

Kayl shook his head. "You've got a mess to clean up first."

Rikkard raised an eyebrow. "What are you talking about?"

Kayl pointed at the researcher. "He's seen your face. You have to kill him."

Rikkard stepped back, dumbstruck. "What?"

"You have to kill him, or he'll be able to describe you to the authorities." Kayl stared at him nonchalantly, as if taking another man's life was nothing.

Rikkard glanced between the researcher and Kayl. "I can't."

The researcher stared wide-eyed, and trembling. "P-Please, don't kill me! I did what you want! I won't tell anyone! I won't, I promise!"

Kayl sighed. "If you can't do this, you won't be able to cut it with the Legion."

Rikkard froze. The Legion was his way out. His way out of everything. If he didn't do this, would Eria go back on their deal? They were smugglers, after all.

His mind flew in every direction. If he killed this man, everything would be solved and he could go on with his life. But, if he didn't, he'd go to prison. There was no denying that, no getting around it.

He had to kill this man.

Cold seeped into his limbs. His finger twitched on the trigger of his pistol. He flicked off the safety. The charging whine filled the silence.

"No! Wait!" The researcher scampered back against the counters lining the wall. "Please!"

Numb spread from his fingers, up his arms and into his chest. Though his heart thumped wildly, all heat fled him. He had to do this.

Rikkard raised the gun to the man's forehead.

This was the only option. The only way out.

His fingers tightened on the grip.

"Do it!" Kayl snapped.

Rikkard closed his eyes and squeezed the trigger.

A loud thump broke the quiet left by his pistol. His fingers felt so heavy he nearly dropped the gun.

"Alright, good. Let's go." Kayl turned to the exit.

Rikkard opened his eyes. The researcher stared unseeing up at the ceiling, a hole burned through his forehead. Much cleaner than the mess of bodies by the elevator. Almost peaceful. It had to be quick. Painless.

He stepped away from the body, and followed Kayl to the exit.

The familiar stench of Radley's filled his nostrils like home. Did all bars smell the same? He wrinkled his nose and rubbed the stubble along his jaw. It had only taken a couple hours to fly back to Bakura, giving him plenty of time to think. Although, he'd done everything in his power not to. He pushed the researcher's face out of his mind and concentrated on the mission, focused on flying and following Kayl until they got back.

Inside Radley's, the myriad of unpleasant smells sent all thoughts of the researcher from his mind. If he closed his eyes, he'd truly believe he was back at Jules' Tavern.

Kayl stopped at the back booth. The same cloaked figure sat within.

"We got it." Kayl set the case on the table.

Eria's lips twisted in a mischievous smile. She flicked her hood back before opening the case. The same mass of boosters lay within. Her grin spread to reveal perfect teeth.

"Good. Very good." Eria closed the case and stood. "You've done well, Rikkard."

Rikkard nodded.

"Welcome to the Smugglers Legion." Eria extended her hand.

Rikkard took it. They shook hands, and Eria sat back down, motioning for them both to sit with her.

Only a day ago he'd found out about the Legion and set off to join them. Now, he was one of them. But after fleeing home, scouring the desert, fending off a pickpocket and killing countless innocents to get this position, was it all worth it in the end?

He hoped so.

Katherine Bogle is a Canadian science fiction and fantasy author. Learn more at katherinebogle.com

UNTIL TOMORROW
TAYLOR HONDOS

I waited. All I ever did was wait. I waited for life to happen. I waited for love to happen; it never did, and it never would. That's why I was here. That's why I was always here with Abraham.

I groaned when it was necessary but other than that nothing. I groaned more out of frustration than satisfaction. I waited for him to be done and off me. I was bored. I was always bored in this moment. My thoughts were always left wandering for some entertainment.

Come on, are you done yet? Can he tell I really don't care about this? Abraham finally cried out, and I sighed in relief but he was too distracted and fatigued to notice.

"Lizzie, baby. How was that?" he asked between ragged breaths. I smiled over at him as he rolled off me.

"Great," I said simply.

"Yeah, I thought so." He leaned over the side of the bed and reached for his shirt. *Thank god. You're leaving.* "I have an early morning tomorrow." *Please don't talk about work right now.* He smiled at me and I tried my best to give a look that didn't show my relief.

96

"Great," I said again. He leaned over the bed and kissed me once on the cheek before grabbing his jacket off my desk and shutting the door behind him.

I rolled my eyes and grabbed my underwear off the floor. I was so sick of this. I let Abraham come over to have sex and then I just let him leave. There was no depth to that man.

I know what you're thinking. What a freak? She hates sex. No, I hate sex with idiots. I hear sex is supposed to make you feel fireworks, emotions, something. I feel nothing. The movies fill our heads with lies about love and sex, and I was foolish enough to buy into it.

When I had sex the first time I was sixteen. I thought to myself, "it's because you're too young. You don't know what love is." That's not true. I still don't know what love is even after all of these years. I don't know what emotions sex is supposed to provoke.

Love isn't real. It's not. I won't ever find it. When you feel less, you have less to lose. This is the motto I live by. It's what keeps my head afloat, and what keeps me from falling into any traps.

I hoped my roommate didn't notice Abe leaving; she would freak the hell out on me if she saw him leaving yet again. I can always feel the judgment rolling off of her when I tell her about my relationship with Abe.

Let me be clear, I've only had sex with a few guys; only two of them meant anything to me. The first guy was when I was sixteen, and we even dated for six years. I was in high school and was a hopeless romantic. I foolishly assumed we'd be together until sixteen turned to sixty. Then I stayed single for quite some time. I didn't do the one-night stand thing. I didn't do any of that. But then I met Abraham.

Abraham had this confidence about him that just seemed to radiate off him. We dated for a few months, but he was too serious. Never joking, never laughing. I want someone to laugh with, not talk about politics and guns at the late hours of the night. Abraham is great. I mean, really, he is. But I don't feel he is my one true love. Sometimes I wonder if something is wrong with me.

I stepped into the shower and felt the heat radiate around me. I looked up at the water spraying down and let it wash over me. Rain. Here it was; it was splashing over me. It was washing over all the things I wanted to be taken away from me. I felt more right here, looking up at water, than when a nice guy was inside me. This was my rebirth every morning.

"We have a new intern coming, Liz." *Fuck.*

My boss, Matthew, was speaking to me and I tried my best to act a little enthusiastic. "Oh, great." I smiled and he scowled.

"Lizzie, when you finish training this intern," He paused, and I held my breath. "You get to move up to full time employee." I was about to scream with excitement.

"Stop it. What?" I practically shouted. "You're giving me the job then?" I was smiling so brightly, my face was hurting.

"Lizzie, you have been the most promising intern we have ever had. The job is yours."

I felt like crying. "Well, I have been an intern for a year now." I smiled brightly and he smiled back.

"You deserve this. Make sure you train him right."

"Okay, will do." He walked away with his limp and I smiled at him. Someone believed in me.

I was finally moving up in the world. When I graduated college six months ago, I was an intern with Matthew's company. He told me that a job would be waiting for me somewhere, someday. He'd never promised me a job here, but I still hoped that he would offer me one.

After my six months was up, I went out in search for jobs, but they said I needed three to five years of experience. It was bullshit. So I signed on to be an intern for one more quarter and look at me now. I was paid very little but I got by.

I continued on with my day. Making phone calls, writing emails, editing the emails before sending them off, organizing, researching. Now I was off on the coffee run. My pumps slammed into the ground as I hurried along the narrow sidewalk. Finally, I reached the coffee shop.

When it was my turn, I turned on my charm for Carlos, who was hella cute, I might add. "I need five soy lattes, one caramel Frappuccino and one cinnamon dolce latte," I ordered and beamed at him.

"Let's not forget to add five pumps of raspberry in a vanilla bean like every other sorority girl." A man behind me mimicked, I held my breath. *Are you fucking kidding me?* I rolled my eyes but my stomach did a strange pull at the gruffness in his voice.

"Have a problem with my order?" I whipped my head around and stopped cold. He was a scruffy looking thing. He smelled mildly of musk. He had big, blue eyes. His curly hair was in full bed head mode.

"Nope. You're just like every other sorority girl. What? Bringing those to your scrapbooking party?" I scoffed and handed the money over to Carlos, who watched with wide eyes.

"Keep the change." He smiled at me but his eyes were still wide. He knew I was capable of going into full bitch mode. He could see it all over my face. And, he had seen me on my worst days.

I yanked my purse off the counter, avoided the beautiful eyes of the rude stranger and walked over to wait for my order. He ordered his order in a soft voice I couldn't hear so I examined his clothes from afar.

He had a scarf around his neck because the weather this time of year was ridiculously cold. He wore timberland boots and tight jeans. He looked like one of those sleepy head ads and I felt heat rushing to my face at how sexy he was. I looked away fast so he didn't catch me staring and get the wrong idea. Hell, I was getting wrong ideas just looking at him.

I felt him beside me before I even looked up. There was tension in the air. We didn't speak. I felt rage because of what he thought of me. He saw me the way everyone saw me. No matter what I did, I was always the little rich girl. I was ungrateful and everything was handed to me. It wasn't that way, but it didn't stop them from thinking that way.

"So, I take it you take your coffee extra hot." His voice broke through the silence. I could feel him still mocking me. It's damn coffee, for God's sake.

"What exactly do you want? Do you want to bug me? It's working, trust me." I scowled and turned away.

"Feisty. I like it." I frowned. Why was he speaking to me if he was just going to be unfriendly?

"Why don't you just go away?" I asked as calmly as possible.

"Cause it's too much fun standing here, annoying you. Plus I'm waiting for my own order." He smiled and I felt my insides flutter. With rage, of course. *He wasn't good looking, or kind of driving my heart wild*, I had to keep lying to myself.

"Five soy lattes, one caramel Frappuccino and one cinnamon dolce latte." *Finally*, I wanted to scream.

I grabbed them all, thankful they provided me with my drink trays, and high tailed it right into the front door as it was opening, I fell backwards as the coffee flew through the air and onto me. The coffee spilled down my shirt and oh, how it burned. "Fuck." I said through gritted teeth, as Carlos came running to my rescue.

"Are you okay, Liz?" He paused when he saw the front of my shirt. My white shirt, I might add. That was see through now, I knew it from his intake of air. "Ouch," he said while looking away and handing me tons of napkins.

I heard his laughter before I could even turn. "Way to go, sorority." He stepped over me and out the front door.

Fuck this day. Fuck that asshole.

"You're late... oh... what happened?" My boss asked frantically when he saw the state I was in.

"Can I go home and change? Or go home and regain my composure?" I said slamming down the cups. "Oh, and here's your coffee."

"Oh, goodness," he said softly. "Aren't you glad that you get to make someone else do the coffee runs for you? But Lizzie, you can't go home. Not today. In ten minutes, Will and Al will be here to discuss strategy for this month. You can't leave. Here, follow me." I grudgingly followed behind him.

"Sarah!" he yelled. I had a towel from Starbucks covering my front side. *Oh damn it,* I scowled. He was getting help from his wife.

"Yes, Matthey poo." Sarah sang through the air. She stopped fast when she saw me, blushing. "Ahem, yes?"

"Oh, Sarah," he laughed. "Do you still have your extra set of work clothes in your drawer?"

"Yes, why?" she asked as if it were normal to have a closet in your desk.

All I did was remove the towel and she was in action, running for her things. It was like she was ready to give someone a makeover. Oh fuck. I was the one in need of a makeover.

"Darling, come with me. We will fix you all up." She turned to her receptionist, "David, take messages for all my calls. This is an emergency." And she rushed off with me.

Sarah was not a busty woman, where I was. So my boobs were hanging out of the shirt. There was a large opening where the button at the top wouldn't snap. The skirt was super tight, but thank god my tights were unaffected by the coffee.

"Sarah, thanks for the clothes, you didn't have to do my makeup though." I said as nicely as I possibly could. It felt like cake was all over my face. My face felt too tight to even smile.

"Nonsense, darling. I have been dying to get a hold of your gorgeous face since day one. You just toss your makeup on, no skill. Now look at you." She threw her hands up in admiration.

Oh I was looking all right, I couldn't even find myself in there. I looked pretty, but I felt so uncomfortable. "Look at my outfit, I'm too fat for your clothes." *Not to mention, I look like a skank.* I turned to face her. "You're so skinny, Sarah, and I am not."

"Enough. You look hot and that's final," she chirped slamming her makeup kit shut.

"Thanks for everything, I will wash and dry these and bring them tomorrow for you." I smiled at her, trying to sound as appreciative as I could.

"Take your time honey. I have so much, don't worry about it." Yes, she did have a lot of stuff. She was as rich as rich can get.

"Let's get out there before Matthew has both of our asses on a platter." She scurried out of the bathroom and I was left staring at myself. It was all too much. I was used to hiding my curves, but now, they were out in the open. I might as well have a sign that said, "look at my arse." Oh well, who really cares, right?

I wanted to scrub all the makeup off, but Sarah was right, Matthew was waiting. I grabbed my demolished clothes off the counter, and scurried out of the bathroom.

The next thing I knew, I was on my ass on the ground, for the second time that day.

When I saw with whom I had collided, I didn't even contain my anger. "What the hell are you doing here?" I practically shouted.

Sarah turned quickly from her desk and rushed over to

help me up. "Oh god, Lizzie, today is not your day," she said as she grabbed my hand, "Did the skirt rip?" she whispered quickly.

I rolled my eyes and shook my hand from her grip. "What is he doing here?"

He was brushing his ass off and he turned on his killer charm. "Lizzie, is it?" His voice ran through my body until I was left with only chills.

"Lizzie, this is our new intern," Sarah said with an uneasy smile, probably because of my inappropriate behavior thus far with him.

Hell no, stop it. Who hates me up there? I must have lived in another life, and I must have been a real bitch to deserve this.

He extended his hand. "Riley. Riley Gold. Nice to make your acquaintance, Lizzie." He said my name with slight anger that I tried to ignore.

I felt like fainting right then. The boy from the coffee shop was standing right in front of me.

I ran away, I couldn't even pretend to care. I left his hand hanging in mid-air and walked around him. Sarah looked like she would faint from my behavior.

I had to clear my head. He was like a curse. This was my fucking intern? This was what I had to deal with? Someone who hated my guts for looking the way I do. I wasn't having it.

Then it hit me, I could make his little life a living hell here. I could rule him. I could teach him correctly; I would because it reflected on me, but I would make him miserable. No. I couldn't make this a hostile work environment.

Be professional, my heart screamed at me, but my mind was ready for a full on attack. He wouldn't ruin my day. He wouldn't. This was the last stop to a raise, a new life, a new job title. I had to fake it until I made it.

I took a second to recover and then I returned.

Sarah was talking anxiously to the boy. Boy, that's right. That's what he was to me.

"Hello." I said reaching out my hand to greet him properly. "I didn't introduce myself, I've had a trying morning. First, I met this rude asshole at the coffee shop." His cheeks were turning red, but I kept going. "Then, I spilt coffee all over myself because of said asshole, and I had to change upon returning to work." His face was beet red. Good, I was in control.

Instead of him reaching for my hand, he moved a hand through his hair. "Well, said asshole sounds like a charmer. What? Were you embarrassed that you ran into the door to get away from his charm?" he said with a smug look that made me want to smack him silly.

I felt my blood boiling. "No, said asshole was just a big dick."

"Oh, I bet you wonder if it was bi–" He couldn't finish because Sarah cleared her throat.

"Children, children, calm yourselves. You have all day to bicker." She paused and looked between us. I was boring my eyes into his. I had never disliked someone so much in my life. "On second thought, don't bicker. It's bad for business."

She walked away and I scurried after her. "We need to get rid of him. He has an attitude problem." I told her in a hushed voice.

"Lizzie, calm down. You have just met him. He's easy going. He's brilliant, by the way. He's going to catch on so fast." I sighed and she turned to face me, stopping in her tracks. "Lizzie, calm down. Teach him fast and he'll be out of your hair in no time. Give him a chance."

I looked behind us at him, he gave me the haughtiest smile I'd ever seen and I clenched my teeth. I turned back to Sarah to complain some more, but she was already gone. This day was never going to end, was it?

I walked two steps before his self-righteous ass caught up to me. He was like a sad little puppy dog that I wanted to get rid of.

"So what's next? What do I do?" *Eager little one, aren't you?*

"Follow me, stay out of the way and keep quiet." He scoffed and I turned to him.

"What's your name again?" I said, although I was fully aware of his name now.

"Riley." He said simply with that conceited look once more.

"Well, Riley. How do you learn?" He didn't answer right away, but I didn't wait. "You learn by watching. You learn by hearing. You learn by—"

"You learn by doing, genius." He cut me off and I felt my frustration building in the pit of my stomach.

"I'm your boss today. And everyday until you get the hang of things, so what I say really goes. Got it?" I asked him quickly.

He nodded slowly, and I pointed to the lockers. "Go put your things up in a locker. Label it with your name and meet me back here in five." I walked away fast to my desk, and I heard him sigh. Maybe I was being too harsh, but he hadn't been kind to me that morning. All I did was order coffee, and he was there to say harsh things. It wasn't him, but it was the words. They brought up memories of the past. Memories I'd buried with my old self.

My old self, I tried to forget her every single day. She was kind. She wasn't brave. She let people walk all over her sorry ass. She had a boyfriend, a good one, or so she thought. His name was Keeton.

It started out good. Of course it did, all relationships start out great. Hopeful. Sexy. With promise. I loved the beginning of a relationship, right before the two partners fuck things up royally.

My old self asked and said the dumbest shit. "Did I do

this okay?" "Do they like me?" "Oh she hates me." The best one was "I'm sorry." No matter if I did it or not. Let me warn you, saying "I'm sorry" transfers all the power to the one on the receiving end.

I hated confrontations. I hated fights. I didn't cuss. I let others run all over my heart. I should have let them run over my mouth so I would shut the fuck up instead.

I met him and I was that girl. The girl who gave into everything. I didn't ask questions. I begged. I begged for him to stay countless times, through tears and high hopes. When he left, I wasn't even surprised but it burned, as Johnny Cash warned me it would.

We dated for six years. Six years of my pathetic life was wasted on a man who said we would be married that fall, but that fall he fell for someone else. I was angry at first. I was upset. I was ruined. I decided it was me; I did this. I wasn't skinny enough. I was too kind. That was why he left. He needed someone brave; someone who wasn't afraid to go out in public because she was afraid of what people were saying about her when she walked past them.

After I'd changed every aspect of myself to win him over, he was already spoken for by the one he cheated with. It wasn't me: it was him. It's always them—the cheater. They could have everything, but they'd still wander. Their minds would still linger on another woman. Not all men, but men like him; the ones who seem too good to be true. They're the ones you have to watch. Take it from me.

My point is I'm not her anymore. I don't care what people think as much as I did. I still will, of course, you can't shut it completely off but I was no longer kind. I was angry. I was no longer shy, I was confident in the fact that I didn't need approval to survive anymore as I once did.

That's why I shut down. Men didn't create that patter in my heart anymore. Nothing caused me much joy. I had sex, but it never meant a thing. It was just something to do. I was closed off, for good. I don't blame Keeton, I thank him for shutting down the hurt in me.

Riley was the opposite of my guy. He wasn't kind. He wasn't trying to hide under the good boy look; instead he rocked the bad boy look. He frightened me a little more than my ex did. He scared me because he didn't hide who he was. He was out in the open. He was like me, now. I let my emotions rule my every move. My anger was my armor, my clothes, if you will. My sexuality was my hair, wild and untamed, and my insecurities were stuffed inside like they were in my purse.

"What are you doing?" His crisp voice spoke through me instead of at me, "you said to meet you over there in five, but you're sitting here twirling your hair." He looked at me questionably.

"I was trying to give you time to process the work environment." Asshole, I wanted to add, but I didn't. "Let's get going." I shoved my chair under the desk and walked ahead.

Do you ever feel people staring at you, and there's nothing you can do but walk on? Well, I wasn't one of those people. I liked to call people out on all of their bullshit, point blank. I felt him staring, at my ass. To be honest, normally I felt super uncomfortable, but I felt myself add a little sway in my step and I heard his gasp. Sarah did give me a super tight outfit. I should work it, right?

"Are you staring at me back there?" I looked over my shoulder to meet his wide eyes and a red face. "You sure do blush an awful lot," I added with a snicker.

"So do you," he said in a matter of fact way.

"That's because you make me angry. You're trying to get a rise out of me here, it won't happen," I refuted.

"Oh really, I think I could think of a thousand ways to get a rise out of you." His voice turned low all of a sudden, and I felt my steps slowing. My heart started to patter slightly. *What was that, Lizzie? Focus.*

"It won't work." He grabbed my arm to stop me, and I

felt my heart do that strange ass flutter again.

"I want to start over. I don't want to be miserable here. I need this job, please," he pleaded, and I saw it then. Sincerity. I'd seen it more than once on Keeton. I wouldn't be fooled again.

"I don't know why you were so unkind this morning in the coffee shop," I said simply.

"It's just the way I am," he merely stated, and I rolled my eyes.

"That's it? That's all you have to say for yourself?" He nodded. "Then I don't care about your time here. You didn't care about my time this morning. Follow me." I turned on my heel sharp and we made it to the meeting room, where everyone was waiting for me. "Stay silent, got it?"

We walked into the room and all eyes were on me. "Matthew, Kyle, Terry, Gerald, Ford," they all smiled at me and I smiled back. "This is our new intern, Riley."

Riley stood impassively and I felt nervous that he was going to make a fool of himself. After a moment of silence, he turned to me and said, "Oh, can I speak?" I felt my blood boiling. I nodded tightly and he was all smiles and talking about the games in no time. I rolled my eyes.

"Okay fellows, let's get down to business," I said with a slight frustrated nod.

"See, look at her initiative." Matthew nodded at me and I beamed. "She's going to make a wonderful addition to us, don't you think boys?" Yes, I would be the only female in the room.

There was an enthusiastic, yes, among the crowd but Riley stood frozen. "Riley, you're lucky to be trained by our best employee/intern."

I laughed, "Matt, you're making me blush." He smiled at me and I felt my skin turning feverish.

"That's the goal, Liz." He reached for my hand and gave it a pat. We smiled at one another and he let go after a moment.

When I looked back up, Riley's eyes were boring into mine. They were intense and I felt myself shying away. Was there anger in there?

"Let's get down to it then?" I asked as a question because I felt nervous all of the sudden. Pressure to be greater than I thought I was. Then there were folders thrown my way, and I gestured for Riley to sit down.

I whispered in his ear, "Okay. This is the folder we have to take care of until the case is done. Which means, don't lose it, and hold onto it as if it were your baby. The only thing I want you to do right now is to listen to everything we say. Take notes in the blank page at the back. Not like taking notes should be that big of a shock or secret." I winked at him.

That's when he leaned in, his tongue brushing my ear. Chills erupted over my entire body. "All your secrets would be safe with me," he whispered back. *What was that? What is happening to you? Chills, really?*

Before I could even comprehend it, we were jumping back and forth with our theories, conclusions and ideas. I couldn't even focus on Riley. When I turned to him, he was sitting there as if nothing happened. As if he hadn't just licked my ear to whisper something that could have been dirty coming from that mouth. His voice. Why was it affecting me so much?

I cleared my throat and got back to work. Writing notes, jumping off ideas with Matt mostly.

That's when Abraham walked in. Abraham, my "sort of" man, I didn't know what he was. In truth, I didn't care much.

"Shit. I'm late." He looked at me and winked. He was walking towards me and stopped dead when he saw Riley sitting in his spot.

His brow was furrowed and I wanted to laugh. "This is our new intern, Riley. Riley, this is Abraham." I said quickly. Riley stood and held his hand out to greet Abe, but Abe just simply stared.

"You're in my seat." Abe said fast.

"Don't see your name on it." Riley countered, and my heart stopped. Abe wasn't the type to like backtalk.

"Abe, chill. Take the seat across from me. You already interrupted us. Sit." I tried to break the tension building between the two men.

Abe duly noted Riley's smug look and continued his walk around the table to face Matthew. I stared at Abe for the rest of the meeting. His stares at me were chilling but I kept my focus on Matthew's voice.

We were in the middle of a breakthrough, and I was busy writing out a plan in my folder, when Riley spoke up. I didn't hear his questions or his thoughts, but everyone was silent. I was gaping at him. He looked at me and shrugged before writing once more.

Matthew was looking angry and I was about to apologize profusely for Riley's behavior, for whatever the hell he said, when Matthew's mouth turned into a beam. "Now you're thinking, Riley. Bravo." He looked to me and gave me thumbs up, like I had something to do with it. I didn't even know what the hell he said, for god's sake.

When I looked at Riley, he was looking down but Abraham was staring a hole through him. Well, this would be fun. My sort of man, Abe, and my hot intern, Riley, going head to head.

After the meeting, Abe grabbed me quick and kissed me on the lips. I was annoyed with his display but I let him. We didn't show affection anywhere but bed, and I was definitely not his girlfriend. So I rolled my eyes and shoved him out of the way, which he probably loved. That's how crazy he was. I walked back to where Riley was still seated.

"Riley," I shouted and he jumped up, grabbing his folder and hustling out of the room. As I was walking away, Abe called out to me.

"Liz, baby, we need lunch," he said playfully, but I was suddenly not feeling so playful. I stopped dead in my tracks at this comment, venom building in my throat. I could feel it.

I turned swiftly, "Then go get your lunch, Abe." His face was a perfect combination of hurt and stun. I thrived on that look. *Keep it coming, Lizzie.*

"Moody as hell," Abe whispered under his breath.

"What was that Abe?" He looked shocked and his lips looked as if they were sealed. "That's what I thought," I said and turned to face Riley, who was still beside me.

Riley was looking between us with a shocked expression. He didn't know what to do, but I could see the ghost of a smile on his lips. I looked him dead in the eyes.

"Let's go before we have to be someone's slave for the day," I said firmly, and he nodded and walked ahead of me. He had no problem following orders. I liked that.

I ended up having to get lunch anyway because Matthew insisted I show Riley the places he would have to venture out to. I cheerfully agreed, but inside, I was mad. I didn't want Abraham to win this war.

Riley was surprisingly pleasant. He took orders for everyone's food, and even ordered it at the shop. He didn't make one mistake. I was slightly jealous because I messed up the first time I order everyone's lunch. We didn't speak to one another, unless it was options for food and where else we ventured out to for lunch.

When we returned, I saw it. Tina with Abraham. I hated that bitch. His other bitch, as I always put it when he brought her up. Yeah, yeah, I needed to respect myself and not sleep with someone who treated me like a piece of meat, as my roommate would tell me. He had many girls. That's the thing, I was allowed one person. And that one person was Abraham. When I decided I was tired of him and wanted to date someone new, he would forbid it. I don't know why I stuck around. Oh yeah, because I don't care about much anyways.

"Your taste in men is impeccable. You pick keepers, I can tell," Riley said as we silently sat the food down in the break room.

"That's none of your concern," I said sharply.

"Why don't you go on a date with a real man?" he asked.

"Oh yeah," I said laughing. "Send him my way if you find one."

"Okay. You're looking at him," he said deadpan.

"Oh where? Under the table, behind door number one? Where?" Frustrated, I slammed the forks down on the table.

"Me." I looked up to find his face without a trace of smugness.

I felt that patter. Fuck that patter. "You? Mr. I Terrorize Girls in Coffee Shops?"

"I was joking with you. I forget you can't take jokes well." He looked away.

"You being unfriendly to people is your idea of joking? Flirting even?" I asked curiously.

"Yes," he said modestly and I felt kind of shocked.

"No," I countered.

"Give me a chance. I'll be the best date of your life." Smugness returning.

"Or the absolute worst date. We hate each other."

"Even better."

"No. Stop it." He frowned. "You're my intern. You and I are nothing. I think you're smart, as does everyone in that room, but you're not nice and let's face it, one of us is going to hurt the other. I'll just say it. I don't get hurt."

He smirked and leaned in and I was reminded of his tongue on my ear. "I don't get hurt either."

"Is that a challenge of some sort?" I said and I leaned into him. He was close to my face. I could move one inch and his mouth would be on mine.

There were footsteps down the hall and we pulled apart quickly. *What just happened?*

"Food!" Ford yelled, and all the others crowded in after him.

Abe walked in hesitantly, staring me down as if he knew something was up. I felt like it was written all over my face, I want to kiss my intern.

I excused myself quickly and ran to my desk. *What are you doing, Lizzie?*

I settled into work and was grateful for the distraction. I didn't know what was wrong with me. Riley was just all shades of wrong for me. Then again, he was cute; he was obviously attracted to me. I was oddly enough attracted to him too.

What if I was reading this all wrong, what if he just wanted to embarrass me more? Why else would he invite me out on a date? He wanted to humiliate me just as he did in the coffee shop this morning.

Anger was rising inside me but I wouldn't let him win this. I would embarrass him first.

I rose up to my feet and when I did, I wish I hadn't. Abraham and Tina were cuddled up in the workroom, which was made entirely of glass. His hand was on her ass, and she was pressed against him as if her life depended on it. That's when he dipped her down into a tight embrace, their lips locked. I shoved my seat behind me and scowled.

His flings were tiresome. If he could have flings, then so could I. I rushed through the building until I found Riley.

"What are you doing?" I asked breathlessly when I found him.

"Uh, organizing files like you told me to. Why? What'd I do wrong now? Did I breathe too heavily?"

I scowled. "Actually, I wanted to take you up on that offer." I smiled as much as I could. *Don't see through me. Don't see that I am using you to make Abe jealous.*

"What offer?" he said with a smirk.

"You know the offer, don't play dumb with me," I said snidely.

"I can't play smart, since I'm so dumb to you. So take it as I'm being myself." He wouldn't look up at me. He kept filing away and I felt my blood pressure rising.

"Seriously, look at me," I said and when he didn't, I knocked his file from his hand, causing the papers to fly into the air.

"Well, that's real mature. Are you sure I'm the younger one?" He smiled and I rolled my eyes. "Actually, I assume we're the same age. How old are you?" When I didn't answer, he smiled. "I'm 24, if you wanted to know."

"You make me act really immature. You kind of drive me insane. Forget what I said. I don't want to take you up on the offer you can't remember anyways," I said softly, and I began gathering the papers on the ground.

"No. Don't. I got it, Lizzie." And he kneeled beside me.

"It's Elizabeth to you, and I want to help. I caused this mess with my immaturity."

"I prefer Lizzie," he said simply and went about gathering the papers with me.

We stood and I handed him the papers, which he stuck into the file before placing it back in the rack.

"Look, do you want to go on the date or not?" he asked me.

"No, I don't want to go. I don't care to go. But I'll go because I want to prove to you how awful it would be."

"Let's place a bet then. If you have a horrible time, you can treat me like shit and make me do unnecessary jobs."

"And?" I smiled at the idea.

"And if you have a good time, you have to stop treating me like shit, and train me to be better than you are at this job."

"What's in it for me?" I said sarcastically.

"There's a lot in it for you, trust me." He held out his hand. "Deal?"

I sighed deeply. Why did I care so much? It would be mindless fun, or mindless torture. Either way, it didn't matter what I chose so I shook.

"Deal."

The day dragged on. Riley and I stayed civil. We only talked when necessary. I taught him what he needed to know for the job, and I counted down until the end of the day.

That was when Abe rushed around the corner toward me.

"We need to talk. Now!" he said quickly, while grabbing my hand. I rolled my eyes and followed him. He pushed me toward the breakroom.

"Explain yourself, now," he said.

"What are you talking about, Abe?" I said softly.

"That new, skinny fucker. What is his deal? And why is he touching my girl?"

"Abe, Tina and you had a tongue session today, and for half of the day, I might add. Don't you have a job to do?"

"So what?" he said seriously. And I stared him down.

"This is over. We are over," I said and his face furrowed, and he looked pained as if he might have a heart attack.

"Lizzie, no. Tina doesn't mean a thing to me." He grabbed my hands, but I yanked them away.

"And to Tina, I don't mean a thing to you either."

Laughter erupted all around me as Abe's friends, Ross and Michael walked into the room.

"Excuse me," I said quickly, to make my escape. I felt the tears coming before I could stop them.

"Lizzie, wait," he yelled but I didn't stop until I reached the bathroom and locked the door. Abe wasn't above coming into the bathroom with me but this time I wouldn't let him. I leaned against the door and cried.

"Lizzie, we have been together for ten months, don't

do this," he shouted through the doors as I crumbled down to the ground.

It was actually eleven months, but I didn't care. I didn't care what he did.

"Leave me alone, Abe. I feel nothing for you. Not even when we have sex. I feel nothing. You mean absolutely nothing. So go mean absolutely nothing to someone else. We're done!" I yelled back.

It was silent and the banging on the door stopped. "Bitch!" he screamed to me, and my heart stopped. There was a large commotion outside followed by a thud, and I gasped, standing quickly.

I yanked the door open to see Riley, holding Abe against the wall adjacent to the bathroom. "Is that any way to treat a lady?" he said through gritted teeth.

"Let me go and I won't punch you dead in the face," Abe spewed.

"How about this, don't speak of this again, and I won't tell Tina about how you cheat on her with every girl in the office?" Riley said calmly.

Abe spit through his teeth, "Tina would never believe you."

"Oh no, explain the video clips your so called friends Ross and Michael say they have of you and Ashleigh." Riley smiled as realization spread all over Abe's face.

"Ashleigh too?" I said through gritted teeth.

"Baby, no. Please." Abe tried to reach for me, but Riley pushed him back against the wall.

"Fuck you, Abe," I said quietly.

Abe looked defeated and Riley put him down.

"Well, that's settled. Get lost." Abe was a big guy, muscles everywhere, while Riley was so small and lanky, I had no idea how he picked up Abe with such ease.

Abe scrambled with a scornful look at me, but he left without a word.

Riley was calm. He smoothes his jacket and casually strolled up to me as if nothing had happened at all. He smiled at me and I felt my knees growing weak.

"Well, how did you manage to pick up Abe?" I asked. He smiled at me without answering. "Let's just add more mystery to you then," I said with a smirk.

"Why do you let people treat you so badly?" he asked softly.

"You don't even know me."

"From what I do know, you let people, even me, run all over you." He reached me in a step.

"I don't care. That's my thing. I don't care about anyone or anything." I looked down at my watch and relief spread over me. "It's time to leave. Where do you want to go on this horrendous date? I want to get home to watch Sex and the City."

I gathered all my things and met Riley in the parking deck at the elevators like he told me to. When he pulled up to me in an Audi R8, I about fainted.

"Is this yours?" I said, choked.

"Yeah, you going to get in or what?"

I rushed in and felt the leather. "Oh my god. This is my dream car."

He smiled and we zoomed off.

We ended up at a very high-end restaurant, and as we were seated, I had to ask. "How are you rich? And why the hell am I your boss? I want to work wherever you were to have this." He laughed but didn't answer me.

"Sensitive topic then?"

"Well, sort of." He paused and looked at me thoughtfully. "I'll tell you. My parents left me money." He didn't go on and I rolled my eyes.

"So you're a rich boy then." I sat back and crossed my arms. That explained his "give me" attitude.

"Rich boy. How clever. Never heard that one before." I rolled my eyes.

"Let's just get this over with, why don't we?" His eyes widened and he nodded. He buried his face into the menu.

This was going to be a long night.

"You roll your eyes an awful lot. Is that your clever defense mechanism?" he said softly.

"Actually, yes. It's a habit now, I think," I said bashfully.

"When you blush, I love it," he said simply, sitting down his menu. I looked into his eyes and saw a glint in them. "Tell me about yourself," he demanded gently.

"What's there to tell?" I was saved by the bell. The waitress came for our orders and I was ashamed that I didn't know what I wanted. Riley threw up his hands and winked.

"We will start with Chateau Lafite, then we will both have the lobster dinner." He smiled sweetly at the waitress.

"Riley," I practically gasped, "that wine is like 4,000 dollars."

"I know."

"You can't buy my affection," I said with a smirk.

"It's my father's favorite. I try to get it whenever they have it. It's a silly tradition," he said without looking at me.

"It's an expensive tradition," I added quickly. "Why is it so important to you?"

"My father and mother were gone almost everyday. Whenever my father knew we would all be together for an evening, he would come home with Chateau Lafite every time. It was our ritual." I smiled at that but he shook his head, "enough about me, tell me about your family."

"I have a mother who left when I was six. I have a father who died of cancer three years ago." I failed to mention that Keeton left me the week my father died, taking away some of my emotions for my father in his last days. Selfish prick.

"Oh Lizzie, I am sorry." He nodded, but he didn't understand. No one could.

"It's okay."

"No, it's not." No, it wasn't. I never brought up my family.

We sat in silence for a moment and I had a tiny fear that I had ruined the evening. But then Riley spoke up. "I was twelve when my mother came into the house drunk for the first time. I was thirteen when she beat my father to the ground for taking her vodka away." I felt my heart racing, no. "I was fourteen when she went to rehab. I never saw her again." He paused to look at me. So much emotion in his eyes, I felt my throat constricting. I couldn't speak.

He continued while looking away, "My father is bipolar. He has been in and out of mental institutions for seventeen years. When she left, he left too. It was my last year of high school. I pretended everything was okay. I didn't tell anyone and then I left for school. I never looked back." He finally met my eyes again.

"Where are they? Do you know?" I asked as he smiled at me somberly.

"They are together. I know this because they sent me money. As if their money buys happiness and could possibly make me forget they're gone." I was about to ask how they had money, but he answered it for me as if he could read my mind. "They were both lawyers. They met in law school. I was given a lot of money, Liz. I don't use much of it."

"I couldn't tell," I spoke disdainfully and immediately regretted it.

"Okay, the car was a joy buy. I love cars. I had to use the money for one toy. I never go out to eat, but when I do, I order things I love."

"Like the wine?"

"Like the wine." He smiled at me. I reached for his hand, and he reached too.

"Thanks for telling me that, Riley." I squeezed his hand in mine.

"Thanks for telling me too. Looks like we're a pair of grown orphans. A pair of whiny, eye rolling orphans," he said as he rolled his eyes, to mock me. I laughed, throwing my head back in pure joy. I had felt alone for so long, but here was someone just like me inside, sitting right across from me.

That's when the food came and I laughed more at that dinner than I had the entire year. Abe never took me out. He took me home, and this was different.

When the check came, I reached for it, but Riley was quicker. "No way. This is my treat."

"Like I could afford this with my intern salary?" I said and he laughed, and it made him look six years younger.

When the car was pulled up to the front door, I was so excited. "One day, I want to drive this."

"How about now?" he asked casually and my mouth fell open.

"Are you serious?" I asked.

"Absolutely. Anything to see you smile that big. Don't wreck my baby though," he added and I yanked the keys from his hands, while sticking my tongue out to mock him.

Then I was driving, I looked over to find him gripping the seat so tightly that I could see the whites of his knuckles. "Oh relax, Riley," I yelled over the roar of the engine. I had never felt so alive.

When I reached my apartment complex, I parked the car, and smiled to him. He looked like he would get sick. "Well, you handled that as expected." He snickered.

"What is that supposed to mean?"

He never answered but I smiled at him anyways. "Walk me up?" I asked, with flushed cheeks. I was nervous. That never happened to me.

He didn't speak, but nodded. He looked nervous too. Good. I wasn't the only one. He walked me to the stairs and I walked ahead, letting him get a good view. When we reached the door, I turned and went towards him in swift movements.

"I want to—" I started, but he was way ahead of me.

"Stop there, Lizzie. I want to take things slow. No one has ever done that for you, have they?" he said quietly.

"No, they haven't," I said, feeling the energy draining from my body. He didn't want me. I felt tears. "You don't want me. I get it. I was ugly to you all day."

He grabbed my face, "Lizzie, no. I want you. You have no idea but I don't want to be another lay. I want to stand out. I want to be different for you."

"You already are," I said calmly.

"No, Liz. You don't get it. I want to make love to you. I want it to be when you're ready, emotionally. I want you to feel something."

"I would–" He cut me off again.

"I heard what you said to Abe. You felt nothing. I bet you never have. With me, you will, Lizzie. You deserve love. You deserve happiness."

I nodded into his hands on my face. "Okay. I will do it your way." What if I could never feel those sparks everyone talks about? I didn't say this out loud.

"My way." He laughed. "Lizzie, where have you been? I've waited for someone to understand me my whole life, and here you are."

I laughed. "I don't believe in fairy tales and true love. I don't believe in love at first sight. Or love on the first date, or first day of meeting, Riley."

"Neither do I. We aren't in some teen novel, with sparkly penises." I laughed.

"Oh my god. Shut up. It's sparkly vampires," I said through snickers.

"Same thing, Liz." He laughed and then he was serious again. "Liz, I believe that we are good for one another, even if it's just friends. You're good for my morale. I feel whole right here. I haven't felt whole for fifteen years. I have told no one about my parents until you. That's big. I feel comfortable and whole."

"I haven't felt whole for a long time either." He nodded.

"I know. I'm not asking for love, or anything crazy, we just met, but I want to be there for you. Through anything

I can help you through. Let me be that person that makes you feel whole too."

I nodded. And he grabbed my hand, leading me to the front door of my apartment. "I am going to kiss you goodnight though. Thank you for a semi-horrible, semi-wonderful first date."

I laughed and he leaned into me, hesitantly. I didn't want to ruin the moment, but I grabbed his head and pushed him towards me. Our lips met, and I felt oceans colliding. My heart was pounding and it was as if I could feel his heartbeat too. The kiss was sweet, but urgent and I could feel it deep in my bones. Those fireworks, that never existed until this moment.

"Wow," he said as we pulled away.

I couldn't speak but I smiled, my cheeks flushed.

"This is promising." He kissed me once more, and my heart fluttered. "Goodnight, Lizzie. Until tomorrow." His hair was in disarray from my hands, and he somehow looked even sexier.

"Until tomorrow." I smiled. Even if he broke my heart, even if we were just friends and nothing came from this, I felt something. My heart was not empty and cold as I had originally thought. I was human, and I felt.

Taylor Hondos is the author of the Antidote Trilogy. She is currently working on the third and final book of the trilogy, Corruption. She graduated from The University of North Carolina at Greensboro with a degree in English. She enjoys reading, writing and endlessly searching for books instead of doing "adult things." Learn more at taylorhondos.com

GHOSTS OF THE PAST
MAJANKA VERSTRAETE

Felicia's plan for college was simple. One: study and prepare for every class. Two: go out sometimes, socialize, and have fun. Within reasonable limits. Three: don't tell anyone you can see ghosts. Preferably, don't see ghosts at all at any time during your entire college career.

Of course, that didn't go as planned. From the very first steps she took into Cedarpine Hall, her dorm and new home for the next few years, she felt the all-too familiar tingling sensation on her skin, and goosebumps running along her spine. A ghost was here.

She'd spent years following her dad into haunted and 'supposedly-haunted' buildings, ridding them of the spirits roaming through the rooms; it made it easier for her to tell when a place was haunted or not. Felicia was more than sure from what her gut was telling her that Cedarpine College had at least one resident ghost, and it was making its presence known.

Just my luck. Felicia figured an old and prestigious university like Cederapine would probably have a haunted auditorium, or an old boarded-up building with a few resident ghosts. But her dorm? Her bad karma must be in overdrive.

"Getting nervous?" her father asked when Felicia suddenly stopped in her tracks.

"A little," she said. Her father didn't share her abilities to sense ghosts. While he'd made his living as a medium, he could neither talk to nor see spirits, relying mostly on his daughter for that. When she was younger, he'd forced her into helping him, even though the experience terrified her. Having to see horribly deformed ghouls and trying to reason with vengeful spirits wasn't exactly a good childhood experience. Despite her fears, he didn't stop dragging her along to séance after séance until they had a huge argument about it a few years ago. Their relationship had been strained ever since, leaving her unable to fully trust him. Not after the nightmarish scenes he'd put her through as a child.

She came from a long line of mediums. Her grandmother was one, and even her great-great grandmother had been a famous medium in the Victorian era. Although, now she understood part of why her father was so persistent. Due to the fact her father didn't share any of their abilities, she suspected it had always privately tormented him, perhaps in the same way forcing a lifestyle hunting down phantoms on her had privately tormented her.

To be honest, going to college and moving out was a relief for Felicia. She was glad her father was taking the effort to drive and drop her off, but she would be relieved to see him go. Time and distance apart would be a good break for the two of them.

Her room was located at the end of the fourth-floor hallway. Thankfully, she didn't have that much luggage, which would mean she or her dad would only have to go back to the car about three times. Guessing by the epic amount of stuff the other college students were carrying, she had packed considerably lighter. A guy passed by her carrying four boxes stacked on top of each other, which rather resembled the leaning tower of Pisa. She couldn't help but to suppress a chuckle at the sight, thankful that it was him instead of her.

Felicia reached her dorm room, checking the number to make sure she had the correct room. As the door to her room was already open, she walked straight in. The shivers she'd felt earlier intensified immediately. If it turned out the dorm she was staying in was not haunted, but just her room in particular, then she'd eat a shoe out of frustration.

"Hey," Felicia said to her new roommate. She spotted the girl sitting on one of the beds, legs crossed, listening to music through oversized headphones. Since she could see this girl had already decorated one side of the room with a number of scarce belongings, the other side and bed must be her own. Felicia noticed right away the girl had a similar minimalistic taste as she had. The girl herself had black hair, wore long cross-shaped earrings, and black clothes. Felicia might as well have been rooming with her twin.

"Hey." The girl's lips curled into a friendly smile. It seemed that she too noticed a kindred spirit. "What's up? I already picked a side, hope you don't mind."

"Not at all." Felicia dumped her box on her bed, gesturing to her father, who was following behind her, to do the same. "I'm Felicia Jones. What's your name?" She extended a hand in a friendly, mutual greeting.

The girl inched forward towards Felicia, accepting her hand and shaking it lightly. "Delilah Martins." She gave Felicia a crooked smile. "I think we'll be friends."

Felicia had been somewhat relieved to see her father leave. She would probably miss him in a week or two, but she was glad for some time away from him. It would allow her time to figure out who she wanted to be, rather than being the person he had wanted her to be all these years.

When she headed back to her room, the hallways were

still crowded. People were rushing back and forth, parents were scolding their offspring for not being fast enough, or for being too fast. Felicia inhaled and exhaled the new air, smelling a heady mix of sweat and stress and boxes. A rather disgusting smell to anyone's nose, but a smell she would cherish because to her, it meant a brand new beginning.

"Hey roomie," Delilah greeted her once she returned to their room. "So, what's your story?" Delilah was still in the exact same position Felicia had found her in when they first met, sitting on her bed, cross-legged, except now the headphones were around her neck instead of on her head.

"My story?" Felicia raised an eyebrow, clearly surprised her new roommate actually wanted to know something about her, and so soon.

"I mean, why did you pick this college? What classes are you taking? Have you got a boyfriend, or girlfriend? I don't judge." Delilah waved her hands about while she talked. "What are your life goals? Hobbies? Anything."

Felicia sat down on her bed, her muscles instantly relaxing. For the first time since this morning, she felt how sore she was. The long ride to college had her body exhausted, but her mind was sharp and wide awake.

"I picked Cedarpine because they wanted me. A lot of other colleges didn't." She let out a dry laugh. "Also, it's far away from home, and that's a bonus." She had practically fled out of the town she grew up in. Not just away from her father, but from everything that had happened. Felicia had been through horrible bullying when she'd gone to high school, as many often did. For her, fleeing was a relief. College was a welcome change, full of new opportunities. "I'm taking mostly psychology classes. No boyfriend. No girlfriend either." She ticked off her fingers, keeping track of Delilah's earlier questions. "As for life goals, there aren't any yet. I'm aiming for just trying to make it through college. My biggest hobby has to be poetry. I love to write poems. You're free to call me lame because of it."

Delilah waved her concerns away. "I like poetry. Makes you all kinds of special and stuff."

She couldn't help but laugh at Delilah's latest comment; it was as true as true can be. "Your turn."

"Hm." Delilah licked her lips. "I picked this college because it was one of the few that allowed me to sign up. I saw that they had a good reputation for journalism classes, which basically answers question two. I'm taking journalism classes mostly. No relationship, yet. My life goal is to become a world-renowned journalist, working for The Times newspaper or something. My hobby is photography. There, that about sums it up."

"Are you any good? Your photography, I mean," Felicia asked.

"I'd like to think I'm pretty decent. I took some pictures of Cedarpine Hall when I came in this morning; it was nowhere near as crowded then as it was when you came in. Would you like to see them?"

"Sure," Felicia said, genuinely enthused by the notion.

Delilah took her camera from her desk, heading over to Felicia's side of the room and claiming a spot next to her on the bed. The camera was carefully placed between them so they could both see the screen. Delilah turned it on and started showing Felicia her photographic results. "This was us driving up to the campus." She clicked through the pictures. "This is the entrance to Cedarpine Hall. Looks so old, I loved it."

Felicia nodded, agreeing. The pictures were indeed beautiful. Whenever Felicia took a picture, it was just that: a picture. Delilah's photos looked like she always managed to pick just the right angle, making something look more extraordinary, more alive, more real.

"And this is the hallway downstairs," Delilah said. "As you can see, not a soul in sight. And this is our hallway here…" She paused, her finger lingering above the 'next' button. "Huh. That's weird."

Felicia narrowed her eyes at the picture. It was their hallway all right, complete with wooden-paneled walls and stern-looking paintings. But unlike Delilah's other pictures, which were all crystal clear and sharp, this one had a foggy mist in the background.

"Maybe it's just a little dust," Delilah shrugged, trying to find an explanation for the fog. She clicked the 'next' button and cursed at the next picture. The fog was even more pronounced here. The mist had moved from the background of the frame to the front. It didn't look like a human figure, not yet at least, but Felicia knew it wouldn't take long before it would.

Delilah had caught a ghost on camera.

"I've never had this happen before," Delilah said. "Sorry, you must think I'm an amateur for not noticing this before now." She moved the camera back towards her so she could take a closer look at the picture, frowning at what she saw. "What the heck is this? It's in every picture of our hallway."

Felicia scratched her head. "I have no idea." She could hear the lie in her own words, but doubted Delilah would. Someone who knew her better might, but her new roomie would be oblivious to her deception. "It's probably just some dust like you thought. This place is so *ooooold*." She stretched out the last word, trying to lighten the mood.

"I guess." Delilah pouted, not looking at all convinced. She sighed and put the camera away. "I've got an entire year to convince you of my skills, so I'm not worried." She got up and walked back to her bed, halting just before she reached it. "Oh, right, I forgot." She fumbled through her pocket and took a note out. "Some guys came by and left this here. It's a flyer for a super-duper awesome party tonight on campus. They left one of these in every room."

"A party?" Felicia groaned. "At the risk of sounding boring, I'm not really in the mood tonight. I ran up and down these stairs more than enough for one day. I think I've already surpassed my exercise quota for the entire week."

"Got ya. That's why I've got a way better idea." Delilah actually looked pleased that Felicia had declined the party invitation. "The girl from Room 43 down the hall asked if we wanted to come over. You know, to hang out, chill, and to get to know each other. We could even wear our pajamas. I'm up for it if you are."

Part of Felicia wanted to just crawl in bed and sleep until morning, but this was a new world full of new opportunities, and if she wanted to enjoy them she better not say no to every opportunity that came along. Besides, it didn't sound that bad. Unlike the party. That sounded dreadful.

"All right, sounds fun," she said. "What time?"

"She didn't say. I guess we can just head over whenever we want?"

"Let's go then." Felicia nodded, got up, and dusted off her pants. She was determined to put all thoughts about the potential ghost behind her. She was determined to try to have some fun.

"Hey, Delilah! Nice you could drop by." The girl in Room 43 opened up her door when they knocked. A gorgeous brunette stood there looking like she could've run away from America's Next Top Model. She gestured for the girls to come in. When both girls were inside the room, they could see another girl sitting on the bed to the left – she was a short, chubby girl with pink-dyed hair wearing matching pink pajamas.

As it turns out, Felicia and Delilah weren't the only guests. Two guys were also there. One guy resembled the girl who answered the door with the pink hair. He didn't have pink hair, but his features were similar to hers. He was slightly on the chubby side, with a round face and a short nose. Felicia's assumption was proven correct when the girl in pink interrupted her thoughts and said, "Hey!

I'm Mel. This is my brother Chad, and his roommate Derek," indicating the other guy in the room.

"I'm Delilah, and this is Felicia," Delilah introduced the two of them to the room of people.

"And I'm Sarah," the pretty brunette on the other bed said. She got up and plopped down on the bed next to Mel. Delilah did the same, leaving the only spot for Felicia next to Derek. He was seated next to Chad on the other bed. Felicia sat down, smiling at Derek. When he smiled back, she felt her cheeks going red.

Derek was hot, but not in an obvious kind of way. He looked like the mysterious boy your parents warned you about. The 'bad boy'. He had short black hair, at least two tattoos that were visible to Felicia, and the darkest eyes she'd ever seen. The kind of eyes she could get lost in.

Delilah coughed, interrupting her gawking. Felicia turned to her and saw her roommate's eyes were wide, her mouth smirking. Great. Delilah had seen her obvious drool-gawking on the first good looking boy she'd come across here at campus.

"Chad and I are twins," Mel said, clarifying any suspicions. "We've always done everything together so it's totally strange that we're not doing this together. We're taking different classes, we're in different dorms…"

Chad laughed. "Yes, it makes me nervous to think about not doing things with Mel. But we're here to find ourselves, aren't we? I'm sure it'll work out."

Sarah crossed her legs. "Yeah, at least you ended up with nice roommates." She poked Mel jokingly in the ribs. Despite how different they appeared, Felicia guessed they might get along fine like she and Delilah would.

"Yeah." Chad slapped Derek on the back playfully. "Couldn't have picked better."

Derek smiled. "I'm just not very happy about the building. The company will do fine." Felicia caught him glancing at her while he said that. She could feel herself turning the color of a tomato.

"What's wrong with the building?" Delilah asked, curious.

"Well, Chad here is convinced it's haunted," Derek mused.

Everyone turned to look at Chad, whose cheeks turned a brilliant shade of red. "Yeah, sure, go tell *everyone* I believe in ghosts."

Derek shrugged. "It's not that big of a deal. Ghosts are 'in'. Don't you watch any of those ghost hunter shows on TV? Anyway, go on, tell them why it's haunted."

Chad sighed and rolled his eyes. "Fine. There's this story about a girl who committed suicide here in the dorm. It includes all the typical ghostly legend stuff, so it's probably not true. I only know about it because I'm a huge horror buff, and there is this guy who owns a video store I order videos from…" He paused mid-speech when everyone gave him a weird look. "What? I like VCRs. Some of the oldies you just can't buy on DVD. Anyway," he continued, "this guy went to Cederapine College before, and he told me about the ghost."

"Doesn't every college have its own ghost story?" Sarah brushed it off, clearly not buying it.

"Yes, but this one is set right here in Cedarpine Hall." Derek's eyes twinkled with amusement. "Come on, what better way to start our college career than by telling ghost stories?"

The hair on the back of Felicia's neck stood up. She wanted to run back to her dorm, crawl under the blankets and pretend ghost stories were just made-up tales. That they weren't real. But that wouldn't be fair to Chad, and everyone else would probably call her a chicken. She wondered what karma God she'd annoyed so that her plans for college would be ruined on the first day.

But this was a story, not an actual ghost. She didn't want to have anything to do with ghosts, and she didn't have to. She could just be a regular young adult, listening to a story, getting spooked at the appropriate places, laughing when needed, and then moving on. No need to be awkward. No need to be the outcast again. She'd left that behind, in the past. She was ready to embrace her new self. At least, that was what she told herself when she said, "Let's hear it." A shiver rolled down her spine but she straightened up and ignored it.

Ghost stories can't be told without darkness, a flashlight, and voices sounding like they come straight from the grave. At least, that was Mel's take on it, and they didn't argue with it. Sarah turned the lights off, whilst Mel gave Chad a flashlight that he pointed straight in his face. It made him look like a scary gremlin. His voice was eerily low as he began to tell the tale.

"It all happened about twenty years ago," Chad started. "A girl named Penelope Wheeler went to school here. She was majoring in philosophy, and apparently, she wasn't very pretty. So you can imagine her surprise when the most popular guy on campus, Chris, asked if she could go out with him."

Felicia pulled her knees up, resting her chin on them. She had a feeling she knew where this story was headed.

"When Chris told her he had fallen for her, she believed it. She thought he was sincere." Chad shook his head. "Poor girl was wrong. He only dated her so she could tutor him in a course he was failing. When she did and he passed, he didn't need her anymore." He paused and licked his lips. "But instead of breaking up with her in a proper way, like any decent person would do, he embarrassed her in front of the entire school."

"How?" Sarah asked in a faint voice.

"On Valentine's Day she'd bought him a lot of presents, which included a written heartfelt letter. He accepted the gifts and the letter, and even asked her to a Valentine's Day party that night. She was so happy, so in love." Genuine sadness filled Chad's voice. He was an excellent storyteller. "She put on her nicest dress and went to the party. Only once she got there, all her presents were on display, and people were laughing at them. She didn't understand and went to ask Chris about it. When she found him, he was reading her love letter out loud for his friends, making fun of her. Mocking her."

Chad paused and looked up, his face illuminated by the ghostly glow of the flashlight. "It broke her heart. She couldn't take it anymore. As a result of her humiliation, she ran away from the party. She hoped things would stop there, but they didn't. The very next day, everyone around her whispered behind her back, laughing at her when she passed them by in the hallway. Chris had made copies of her note and had passed it out to everyone he knew. It was the ultimate betrayal. She couldn't deal with it anymore. That same morning, she left her room as she always did; however, she was silent as not to wake anyone. She made her way to the window of the fourth-floor hallway, waiting until she saw Chris approaching. He went for a morning run at six o'clock sharp every morning on campus, always taking the same route." Chad paused for a second, taking a deep breath before continuing .

"Penelope opened up the window and looked down on the ground below. She saw that Chad was coming closer to where she stood above. The morning air slammed into her face, but she didn't feel it's coolness. She didn't feel anything." Chad's voice grew more anxious. Felicia's heartbeat picked up and she clenched her fists. Everyone else seemed equally enthralled by the story.

"She stepped out onto the window ledge and looked down," Chad said. "She screamed his name. *Chris! Chris!* He looked up when she called out his name, his eyes instantly widening." Chad paused and glanced from Derek to Felicia, to Delilah, Sarah, and Mel. "Then she... JUMPED!" He shouted the last word.

Mel screamed and Sarah yelped. "Oh my God, don't do that!" Mel said as she slapped her brother on the knee.

"You idiot!"

"Sorry." Chad grinned. "I couldn't help myself."

Felicia unclenched her fists. During the story, she'd dug her nails into her skin without realising she'd done so. The story had her quite worked up, so she took a deep breath to calm herself. Delilah and Derek were the only ones who didn't seem spooked by Chad's outburst.

"Come on, tell the rest of the story," Mel said, gesturing for her brother to continue.

Chad lowered his voice again. "Penelope passed away, lonely and betrayed. Chris quit college immediately, moving to a different state. But that wasn't enough for Penelope. Her spirit is still here, haunting Cedarpine Hall. Many people have apparently seen her jumping from the fourth-floor window, even 20 years after it actually happened. She always screams *Chris!* Then she jumps."

Everyone stayed quiet for a minute, then Sarah let out a nervous laugh. "Quite the story. But isn't it a little convenient that he just happened to take the same route every day?" She giggled, shrugging. Felicia, however, hadn't missed the slight tremble in Sarah's voice.

"Some people are like that," Mel said. "Creatures of habit. I feel bad for Penelope though."

"If she was even real," Derek said. "I mean, it's just a story. Every university has one of these urban legends."

"It's real." Delilah held up her cellphone. Felicia hadn't even noticed that she'd dug it out. Delilah had already done a search on Penelope's legend.

Delilah showed them an article. "When Chad mentioned Penelope, I was already digging. Says so right here, 'Penelope Wheeler committed suicide by jumping out of a fourth story window of Cedarpine Hall.'"

"Show me." Sarah grabbed the phone from her. "Oh my god…" her voice trailed off.

"This explains the pictures," Delilah said to herself, sounding suddenly excited. She turned to the others. "I took some pictures in the hallway earlier, and they all had this weird fog on them. I thought it was dust or an error or something, but I've used this camera for years and it's never happened before."

Mel's mouth dropped open. "You caught a ghost on camera! That's freaking amazing. Show us."

"Sure, I'll go get it. Can you put the lights on please?" Delilah put her cell phone back into her pocket. "I don't want to trip over anything on the way to my room with just that flashlight lit."

"Sure thing." Chad got up, since he was the one holding the flashlight, and walked to the light switch. He turned the lights on, causing Felicia to blink several times when the lights blinded her for a second.

"Anyone going to come with me?" Delilah asked, looking pointedly at Felicia. "I *reaaaally* don't want to walk through that hallway on my own now."

No one replied at first but rather reluctantly, Felicia sighed and got up. "I'll go." She didn't want to, not with her hands trembling, and certainly not with the story so fresh in her mind. She'd seen and heard enough ghosts to last a lifetime, but she didn't want to let her new friend go on her own.

Delilah pushed the door open to the hallway, darkness greeting them. The hallway appeared to be completely deserted. Most people had probably gone to the party Delilah had been invited to. Felicia began to regret not going to the party instead.

"We'll be back soon." She didn't know why she said it, but she did. She closed the door behind her.

"Way to go," Delilah said. "You said the exact thing people always say in horror movies *right* before they die."

"I don't watch many horror movies," Felicia said, hoping to sound less spooked than she felt.

Delilah wrapped her arms around herself. The night lights were on and casting an eerie glow over the hallway. If they hadn't just listened to a supposedly true story of a girl's suicide, neither Delilah nor Felicia probably would be as spooked as they were now. Every fiber in Felicia's being was on edge.

Besides, the ghostly sense she had, the familiar tingling feeling on the back of her neck, was on full alert. The ghost Chad had described was real alright, and she felt it was growing stronger every second, which meant that sooner or later, the ghost would make an appearance. That was usually extremely unpleasant for her.

"It's cold," Delilah complained, shivering slightly. "I should've grabbed a jacket."

Felicia nodded, although she doubted a jacket would've done any good. The temperature was plummeting fast.

"Let's get to our room." Her voice trembled slightly, her breath forming a cloud when she spoke. The ghost was gathering energy, pulling it from everything surrounding it in an effort to manifest.

The lights buzzed overhead. Delilah frowned at the noise and looked up. "That's creepy." She looked back at Felicia, looking for assurance. "Maybe it's nothing? Could just be the lights do that all the time."

But this wasn't Felicia's first manifesting rodeo. She felt the eerie sensation lingering in the air, the sense of something growing stronger. The air was charged with electricity, with the promise of something arriving.

"Don't look at me like that," Delilah whined. "You're scaring me."

Felicia didn't care, she just didn't want to be here when that ghost manifested. To Delilah, however, it might just look like a glimmer of smoke or mist, at most a see-through phantom walking toward the window. For Felicia, it would be a full-blown apparition, as real as any human being walking around on campus. The ghost, when fully manifested, could look one of two ways: the way she had in life, a regular human being she could barely tell apart from others. or the way she did when she passed away. Horrible, disfigured, covered in blood. Felicia didn't want to consider the latter option.

"Just hurry," she snapped, half-pushing Delilah through the hallway. They'd barely gotten three steps farther when *it* happened.

The lights went out.

Delilah yelped and grabbed Felicia's hand, the two now standing in dark. "Oh God," she whispered, terrified. In the silence, she let out a nervous laugh. "I can't believe this. The lights have to go out right after we're telling a ghost story." She laughed again. "What a coincidence. Right?" Her voice wobbled.

Felicia pinched Delilah's hand, trying to make her quieten down and comfort her at the same time. "It's not a coincidence."

Delilah was silenced, but not for long. After a few seconds, she spoke again. "Do you think…" She didn't get to finish that sentence. At the end of the corridor, a light appeared. It glowed brighter and brighter with every passing second.

Felicia couldn't move. Her hand was stuck in Delilah's and her legs were frozen to the floor. She always had this reaction when a ghostly presence revealed itself -- the feeling of being paralyzed. It was a moment so profoundly strange, so extremely otherworldly that even though she wanted to look away, she couldn't.

"What's that?" Delilah whispered.

Felicia didn't reply. She kept on staring as the light grew brighter and began to take on a shape. Her heart beat rapidly in her throat. She'd seen dozens of ghosts, but she never got used to it.

"It's… It's Penelope." Felicia's voice was so faint, it seemed to come from another dimension.

The blinding light faded away slightly, leaving a figure in its stead. To Felicia's relief, Penelope Wheeler didn't look like a walking corpse. She looked the way she probably had in life, a regular girl, ordinary and plain except for her face. Her face was a mask of sadness.

"Oh my God, oh my God, oh my God." Delilah

repeated the sentence like a mantra whilst moving towards the wall, pulling Felicia along with her.

Felicia focused all her energy on breathing steadily. The ghost glided toward them, the sadness so enormous it invaded all of Felicia's being. She felt Penelope's grief, and the depth of Chris's betrayal. The feeling was so powerful, her knees buckled. If she hadn't been holding Delilah's hand, she would've collapsed on the floor.

Penelope didn't look at them; she was a residual haunting. She moved past them without so much as a second glance. Every day, the poor girl would be forced to relive her death, creeping through the hallway and jumping out of the window. She continued past them, with Delilah still pulling Felicia along to follow her. Rather than being glued against the wall, they now stood in the middle of the hallway. Delilah's voice had died out, and they both stood speechless.

Penelope stood at the window. She waited. Her presence was one of immense sadness. This was not a malicious ghost like Felicia had faced in the past. Penelope was grief incarnated. She was a person you had to feel sorry for, which Felicia did.

After what felt like an eternity, Penelope opened up the window. She looked down, crying out "Chris!" The scream that followed was terrible, so full of grief and betrayal that it struck at Felicia's core. She let go of Delilah's hand, shaking and crying, falling to her knees on the floor as Penelope jumped.

The lights immediately turned back on. Noises that had been silenced returned, and the world moved on again. A girl's unfortunate death long forgotten by all but the ghost herself, who was forced to live through it again, night after night. All except anyone who was unlucky enough to see her, or sense her presence.

Delilah bent onto her knees beside Felicia, putting an arm around her shoulders. "Are you okay? Felicia, are you alright?"

Felicia looked up at her, tears stinging her eyes. "Such grief. I don't... I can't... I'm so cold."

Delilah helped her up onto her feet. Felicia leaned against the wall for support, taking a few deep breaths.

"What did you see?"

Felicia's teeth were clattering from the cold. This always happened after she saw a ghost. A medium she once knew had explained to her that ghosts drew energy from the strongest person around. Being a medium, Felicia was nearly always the strongest person ghosts could draw energy from, so they did. This usually left her drained and cold, sometimes physically ill.

"I... An orb of light," Delilah said, her hand still on Felicia's shoulder. "Moving toward the window. Then it disappeared." She frowned. "Why? What did you see?"

Felicia looked her new friend straight in the eyes. This was a now-or-never moment, she knew. All her life she'd been the 'weird girl'. The girl who saw ghosts. Going to college had been her one chance to reinvent herself and to start over, to become someone new, someone delightfully ordinary.

If she told Delilah the truth, she would go back to the person she had always been. Her chances to start anew would be gone. Even if Delilah swore to tell no one else, if anyone knew the truth, she might as well just be the 'weird girl' all over again. Seeing ghosts was part of who she was, but not a part she wanted. It was a part she wanted to shed, like bad braces or funky glasses that got replaced by even teeth and contact lenses. But her abilities weren't as easily ignored.

"Come on, Fel, talk to me," Delilah said, squeezing her shoulder lightly. "I'm worried."

Those big blue eyes stared at her, begging for her to open up. Felicia couldn't lie. She couldn't deny it. What use was making friends if you lied to them from the start? The appearance of Penelope Wheeler proved that she couldn't outrun her abilities. She couldn't deny who she really was. Taking a deep breath, she began to tell Delilah the truth. "I saw Penelope's ghost. Not just an orb, but a real ghost looking like a real person. She opened the window and jumped. She called Chris's name, really loud. She was so sad." She shook her head, thinking about Penelope's grief.

Delilah frowned at her. "What the... How could you see all that? How come I only just saw this light orb..." her voice trailed off.

"Because I've always seen them." Felicia stepped aside, which caused Delilah to let go of her. She straightened her back, preparing to continue. "I've always been able to see ghosts and communicate with them."

She took a deep breath and clenched her fists. "It's who I am. I talk to ghosts. Back in high school, some people called me 'ghost girl' because of it. I wanted to come here to college and reinvent myself. Pretend I was normal. But I'm not. I see and talk to ghosts."

Delilah's eyes widened, not so much at what Felicia had said, but more at something that was clearly happening behind her. Felicia frowned and turned around. Mel, Sarah, Derek, and Chad stood in the doorway of Mel and Sarah's room, and from the looks on their faces, they'd heard everything Felicia had just said.

Felicia swallowed hard, bracing herself for what was to come. Back in high school, her abilities scared people. Most of them stayed as far away from her as they could, acting like she had the plague. Others thought she was just an attention-craving liar, none of which was true. Not many people accepted her gifts, not even her 'friends'. They had been wary of her because she'd seen things they hadn't.

She expected nasty remarks, people telling her to get away from them. She had been willing to tell Delilah, but only because she felt a connection to her, a similarity that went beyond the same taste in clothes. She felt they were kindred spirits. The others she didn't know well enough

140

yet, and she could only imagine how they'd react. But it didn't happen. They didn't turn pale and run away, they didn't call her a 'weirdo' or 'crazy' or anything else. Instead, Mel blinked at her, and said, "Really?" At the same time, Chad laughed and said, "How freaking awesome is that?"

Sarah seemed more timid, less convinced. But she didn't exactly run away either. Felicia felt an arm on her back. Delilah smiled softly at her. "Girl, you're even more amazing than I thought. Chad's ghost story just now must've been so real for you. Do you have any of your own stories?"

"So, you believe me? You don't think I'm making it up just for attention?" Felicia frowned, still uneasy that they took it far easier than she thought.

Delilah shook her head. "Why would I think that? I was here just now, wasn't I? I saw that orb too. If you say saw something more, then I'm all ears."

"I'm not usually a big believer of this ghost stuff," Derek piped up as they all headed back to Mel and Sarah's room. "I'm not sure if I buy all of this 100% yet, but if you've got any good stories to tell, I'm listening."

"I thought you all were going to hate me if you found out," Felicia said. She still didn't quite understand their reactions. "I mean at my high school, people mostly avoided me because of it."

"Ugh, don't talk to me about high school." Chad spoke up, waving a hand dismissively. "Everyone called me fat in high school. They also made fun of Mel and I because we liked doing things together. Getting along with your sibling apparently isn't 'normal'. As if. Screw them, and screw high school." He gave a small, amused laugh.

"I didn't really feel like I belonged there either," Delilah admitted. "People thought it was weird that I liked photography, that I was actually good at it. When I beat the queen bee at a photography contest in my sophomore year, I kissed my social life goodbye."

"Do you want a real sob story?" Sarah asked while she sat down on the bed, crossing her legs. "I used to be one of the popular girls, but this other girl really had it in for me. She kept telling me I was fat, and after a while I started to believe her. Following that, I struggled with anorexia for a few years because of what she said. I'm actually nineteen, but it took this long for me to get my life together again enough that I could head off to college."

"Wow." Felicia let out a breath, genuinely surprised.

"Yeah." Sarah shrugged. "You wouldn't guess it as you see me now, but it was a hard road."

"And I, I had a deadbeat dad. I barely graduated high school. The only reason I'm here is because my grandmother took me in, deciding to give me a second chance. I didn't have many friends in high school either. It's tough to when your dad is the local drunk." Derek added.

"So you see?" Mel said. "I don't think anyone gets through high school unscathed. It's a cruel, judgmental place. Not so here at least. I refuse to let it be that way. We're here to get our fresh start."

"But not by hiding who we are," Delilah said as she put an arm around Felicia's shoulders. "Instead by *embracing* who we are. We're adults now, and this is who we are for better or worse."

Felicia nodded. They were right, and she had been a fool to worry so much about hiding the abilities that made her who she was. "You guys are right."

"Sure we are," Mel said. "But now we've shared all our sob stories… How about you tell us about how you can see GHOSTS." She shouted the last word causing everyone to jump as she began clapping in excitement. "Also tell us what really happened out in the hallway. I want to know that too."

"Well…" Felicia blushed and scratched her neck. "I don't quite know where to start. It's a long story." Chad leaned back and looked at his pocket watch. "We've got all

142

night. Or at least until midnight. I want to make it to class tomorrow morning bright and early."

Felicia smiled and began to tell them her story. For the first time in as long as she could remember, she felt all right with who she was and who she was meant to be. She no longer felt the need to hide her true self. She was becoming an adult, and part of becoming an adult was not reinventing who you truly were, but accepting the things that make you, you.

Majanka Verstraete has written more than twenty unique works of fiction. A native of Belgium, Majanka's novels explore the true nature of monsters: the good, the bad, and just about every species in between. Her young adult books include the acclaimed MIRRORLAND (YA Dark Fantasy) and ANGEL OF DEATH (YA Paranormal) series of novels. Learn more at majankaverstraete.com

STARS AND ATOMS
JANNA JENNINGS

Chapter 1

Adam's hand fluttered to his chest in an unconscious movement he quickly schooled. The invitation was there; he'd already checked it twice since slipping it into the inner breast pocket of his tux.

The movement did not escape the notice of Bruner who cocked an eyebrow at him as if to say, *relax,* as he led Adam down a sterile white hall. After a week in mandatory quarantine with the guy, Adam knew almost nothing about him. Any personal inquiries were dismissed with monosyllabic answers, or more often than not, the quirked eyebrow. Any questions pertaining to the invitation in Adam's pocket were treated to the curt, but predictable, "That is outside your time experience" response. Adam was beginning to think Praetorian training included some mild brainwashing.

Despite his retired heavyweight boxer appearance, Bruner had more years of schooling than a brain surgeon. In a job that Adam viewed as a hybrid of CIA agent and Indiana Jones type historian, it was up to Bruner to ensure his clients made their trips in one piece. His employer, Era Excursions, didn't relish leaving the timeline rippling in their wake. That was the one piece of information Bruner hadn't minded sharing during their week of bonding.

The Praetorian held up his hand in a clear military command to halt as he checked a corner before motioning Adam after him. Adam managed not to roll his eyes at the dramatics. The bowels of EE headquarters were deserted except for the hiss of scrubbed air through the vents high on the wall. The time traveling company was serious about the well-being of the timeline, and that included not dragging germs between the decades like a snotty toddler. The CDC would have a heyday if someone infected the greater Los Angeles area with the Spanish flu of 1918. Thus the mandatory quarantine.

Not for the first time, Adam let the few details he knew about the trip tumble through his brain, hoping this time to twist the facts in an order that made sense.

1.   An invitation had arrived a month ago from a Mr. and Mrs. Gregory Julian announcing the pending marriage of their daughter, Julie Ann (Julie Ann Julian? Really?) to a Mr. Miles Rutherford. The invitation was addressed to him: Adam Edelstein. This was not a mistake. Adam had asked.

2.   Adam knew none of these people.

3.   The wedding date and location were listed as October 6, 2070, Beverly Hills, California.

4.   Today was September 7, 2016.

5.   His trip to the future had been paid in full.

The arrival of this invitation had obviously resulted in a few questions. The biggest of all, who wanted a nineteen-year-old quantum physics major at their wedding?

The invitation had been hand delivered by Bruner himself a month ago. Mail from the future wasn't unheard of, just very rare. Adam had looked into it once, just out of curiosity, and when he learned that postage sold for the same price as a new SUV, he laughed at himself and closed down Era Excursions' webpage. Who would ever pay that? Especially since you couldn't write things to your past self like, "Don't buy that house," or "you'd be a fool to pass up that job," or the one Adam would have written to his seventeen-year-old self, "don't give that girl another glance." The edict had been in big, bold letters across the top of the webpage: *TAMPERING WITH THE PAST IS STRICTLY FORBIDDEN*. Underneath it, in a slightly less forbidding font: *All mail is read and censored when necessary.*

Who in their right mind would spend the equivalent of two years rent in LA to send a complete stranger an invitation to a future wedding?

That had been one of the questions that had triggered Bruner's automatic response. Now Adam felt, "That is outside your time experience," was his personal catchphrase.

Not only that, but to pay for his trip in *full?* Adam had asked how much a trip fifty years into the future generally ran, but Bruner had demurred on this point as well, and the internet was no help either. Apparently, you had to set up an interview with EE to get a personal quote. So Adam was left imaging the worst.

The entire situation was accordingly disturbing, the circumstances so strange, Adam felt like he was being drawn into an H.G. Wells novel and balked at the idea of accepting.

Bruner had made a face like he was dealing with a spoiled child. "What exactly is the problem?"

"I don't know these people; a situation *you* refuse to be helpful in."

Bruner waved away his objections. "I would never allow a client into unsafe circumstances. Praetorian's take an oath. That is not a logical protestation."

"It's not about safety." Not entirely anyway. "It's about comfort."

"Time travel is not uncomfortable," Bruner said.

"Not that kind of comfort—" Adam sighed. He'd never been good at explaining things. "I won't know anyone. I'm afraid I'll feel... obligated."

And it had appeared, the first of many cocked eyebrows. "Obligated to do what?"

Adam raised his arms in frustration. "I don't know!"

They'd come to the end of their wanderings under EE headquarters. Ultimately, Adam had agreed to go and the reason was behind the blank, white door Bruner was currently blocking with his NFL-sized shoulders.

Adam made it very clear to Bruner when he accepted the invitation why he was doing so. Any quantum physics student would give up his full ride to MIT to see the technology, to touch it, to experience it first-hand. A glimpse at the not too distant future was just a bonus. The wedding, hardly a footnote.

Bruner motioned Adam forward. The boy bit back his impatient sigh and spread his arms and legs like he'd been selected for extra screening at the airport. Adam had been warned any metal on his body could have catastrophic effects during time travel, and he'd already checked himself several times, but Bruner patted him down anyway. He made him turn out his pockets, checked his shoes, and even bent back his ears to check behind them. The Praetorian's grunt of satisfaction--that from anyone else would have been a loud, "Ah, ha!"--when he examined Adam's glasses made his heart sink.

"They're plastic," Adam protested.

"The screws aren't," Bruner said, squinting at the centimeter of metal that held Adam's glasses together. "They'll have to stay."

"I'm practically blind without them."

Bruner shrugged. "We could get plastic screws for

them, but then we'd be breaking quarantine, which would mean another week in the isolation chamber…"

"Fine, fine. Leave them here," Adam grumbled, pinching the bridge of his nose in irritation.

Bruner slid the glasses in a cubby next to the door and pressed his palm to a security plate. The door slid open. Adam's breath hitched in his throat. Finally, the time machine.

"Is this a joke?" Adam asked. The room was just as empty and sterile as the hallway. He spun around, landing his glare on Bruner. The Praetorian's face was split in a grin, a rare show of any emotion.

"Not a joke, but the look on a first-timer's face is always good for a laugh."

Bruner led the way to the center of the room where a polished disk, three feet in diameter, was set into the center of the floor. Adam shuffled over and poked the toe of his black Converse at it. The surface was… odd. He bent to get a better look and run a hand over it, unable to identify the alloy it was constructed from. It was hard as steel but somehow watery, or slippery may have been a better description.

"Step on," Bruner instructed, extracting a small, black key fob from his pocket that looked exactly like the one to Adam's used Ford Fusion.

Adam eased a foot onto the disk. It was almost like stepping on ice, but not quite. Maybe liquid mercury? But who in their right mind would make something like this out of that toxic substance?

"I can't figure out what it's made of," Adam said, tightening his little-used ab and leg muscles just to keep his footing.

"That's because the material hasn't been invented yet," Bruner told him.

"I don't suppose you'd tell me—" Adam began.

"That is outside your time experience."

But this time Adam detected an amused undercurrent

148

embedded in the phrase. The man seemed to be toying with him.

Bruner followed Adam onto the disk and tapped a button on the key fob. With a faint beep, the disk under his feet vibrated, then the walls began to move.

Adam sucked in a breath and involuntarily eased closer to Bruner, almost losing his footing in the process. No, the walls weren't moving. Were they? Adam glanced down and almost lost his lunch from the wash of vertigo. He was pretty sure they weren't moving, and the walls weren't moving, so what...

Something was gathering around them. Without his glasses, the best he could make out was an insubstantial mist that wafted from hidden corners of the room. Vaporous and dark, the substance accumulated, blocking out the walls until they were gray ghosts.

This time Adam's movement toward the block of muscle that was Bruner could not in any way be construed as involuntary. He was seconds away from grabbing the man's beefy bicep like the clueless blonde in a horror flick when Bruner decided he'd suffered enough.

"No reason to worry, Mr. Edelstein. All standard procedure."

"What is it?" Adam asked, shrinking away. But if there was one thing he could count on, it was his science-driven brain taking over. Just as quickly, he was reaching a finger toward it, his apprehension taking a back seat to his curiosity.

"An electron diffusion region is forming," Bruner replied. "They're also known as--"

"x-points," Adam breathed, watching the darkness gather. "Where the magnetic field of the earth connects with the magnetic field of the sun."

"Very good, Mr. Edelstein," Bruner intoned, as if Adam were a first grader who'd properly identified the difference between a solid and a liquid.

Adam ignored his tone. "X-points are invisible. Their

existence was only proven a few years ago." He glanced at Bruner as if he might be pulling his leg. "They're impossible to predict or find. There have been some theories they could create uninterrupted paths between great distances. Portals some call them. How... "

The loss of Adam's glasses made Bruner's face little more than a smudge in the gathering darkness. He didn't even bother with the edict this time, just that damned cocked eyebrow and a smug smile.

"They only occur naturally," Adam tried to argue, but with whom he wasn't sure.

"They did," Bruner replied, nearly jovial at the sight of Adam's world being turned upside down.

Chapter 2

The hole of darkness gathering in front of Adam and Bruner was solidifying. Curiosity had morphed into excitement for Adam, leaving any misgivings far behind. Hole wasn't really the best description Adam realized. It was a sphere. Just like Einstein had predicted. A perfect ball of oblivion.

If Adam had been asked yesterday if he knew what nothing looked like, he would have said sure and riffled through mental images of empty rooms, skies bleached of color or clouds, and nights so dark you couldn't see your hand in front of your face. But staring into the forming wormhole, Adam realized he didn't really know anything about nothingness. He couldn't begin to explain the complete lack of substance he was facing. Before, there had always been something in the emptiness, even if it was just the invisible oxygen mixture that made up earth's atmosphere. With the fully formed wormhole in front of him he imaged this is what death felt like to an atheist.

"A few deep breaths will help," rumbled a voice next to him. So completely absorbed with the wormhole in front of him, Adam had forgotten about Bruner. He nodded, his gaze steady on the phenomenon inches from his face.

"On three, then. One. Two. Three." Bruner and Adam stepped as one into the nothingness. As his body melded with the empty black space, it never occurred to Adam not to step into the oblivion. Even if death had greeted him on the other side, he wouldn't have hesitated. Any scientist would understand. There was nothing greater than to *know*.

An immense pressure squeezed Adam, like needing to pop his ears, except the feeling was all over his body. Inside the wormhole circles of colored light lined the nothingness, making it feel like a tunnel.

Einstein rings, Adam thought when he found he could form no words while in the wormhole. He'd seen the phenomenon once when a friend let him peek through the lens of the Griffith Laboratories million dollar telescope. Rare, but not unheard of, these circles occur when light comes in contact with something so massive, like a black hole, it actually bends from its naturally occurring straight line. Adam looked around the wormhole with a new level of wonder, spotting for the first time their destination. Like looking through a glass sphere, the image was warped and unevenly magnified. Without his glasses, it took a moment for Adam to identify a room, identical to the one they left.

The end of the x-point didn't so much approach as swallow them whole, spitting Adam and Bruner out the other side. Adam lost his footing, landing on all fours on the cool bleached floor, content to hug something solid and gasp for a second. His heart felt like he'd just jumped off a bridge without a bungee cord.

The recycled air wheezed quietly overhead as Adam slowly raised his head. Bruner had remained on his feet, the man looking as ruffled as a blackjack dealer who knew all the cards.

"You said," Adam panted against the floor, "time travel. Wasn't. Uncomfortable."

"Do you feel discomfort?" Bruner asked.

Damned that eyebrow.

"I've never felt so." He extended a hand to help Adam to his feet. "Everyone is a little different, I guess."

"You guess," Adam snorted, his muscles making *their* discomfort loud and clear. A few breaths bent over his knees and he was able to straighten up. "Are we still at Era Excursions?"

"Of course. The electron diffusion region only allows us passage through time, not space," Bruner said, sounding like he was lecturing a five-year-old again.

"Then how do you know we're in 2070?"

"Because I do not make mistakes, Mr. Edelstein," Bruner said, striding toward the door. "This way."

Instead Adam bent down and passed his hand over the odd metallic plate again. What he wouldn't give for a sample of the alloy, MIT's top notch lab equipment, or just a laptop for pity's sake. Adam stood, glancing into the corners of the room. Where had the x-points originated from? Did the electrons collect from the room? Or where they--

"Mr. Edelstein." Bruner managed to roll his name into a gravelly sigh.

Adam gave the nearly bare white room a longing look before following the Praetorian through the sliding door, into the hallway that he felt he'd left only moments before. He glanced at the cubbies, expecting to see his glasses waiting for him. The cubes were empty.

"Where are my glasses?" he asked.

"Really, Mr. Edelstein, you can't figure that out?" Bruner asked.

Adam glared at the empty cube, trying to reason through it. "Someone moved them over the last fifty years?"

"And who would that person be?" Bruner said, waving Adam forward. Reversing their trek under EE back to the main floor.

"How should I know?"

"Let me phrase it a different way. When we return to your time, what is the first thing you will do when exiting the time traveling room?"

"Get my glasses... oh. I moved them."

Bruner gave him a disappointed look that Adam had seen several times. Each instance was after he'd done something a little... well, absentminded. A look that clearly said, *you* attend MIT?

"Yes. Back in 2016. So why would they be here now?" Bruner continued.

Adam was trying to decide which expression of Bruner's he hated more, the smug look or the raised eyebrow.

The elevator ride out of the basement was silent and uncomfortable as Adam whisked past the isolation level where he'd spent a week of his life, and back to the street level where his journey had begun. All the while he looked for signs that fifty years had really passed him by. Furniture that had appeared, deterioration of the building, anything. But the stark white hall of Era Explorations was so bare, there wasn't much to go on.

The elevator door whispered open, leaving Adam face-to-face with a pleasant woman whose business suit and clipboard lent her an air of authority.

"Welcome Mr. Edelstein." The woman bobbed her head, giving Adam a front row view of the gray roots taking over the severe part in her hair. "I'm Maria Schneider, Director of Era Excursions, Los Angeles branch."

Adam opened his mouth to express his confusion. Mr. Donaldson was the director here, he'd been greeted by him personally when he'd arrived. He snapped his mouth shut just in time to keep himself from looking like an idiot twice in a row. Judging by Mr. Donaldson's age in 2016, he was, in all honesty, probably dead at this point.

Instead Adam smiled and bobbed his head back at her.

"I hope your journey was satisfactory," she said, bustling him out of the elevator, a bemused Bruner in his wake. "We have a car waiting just out front to take you to your final destination." She moved along at a good clip for someone wearing three inch heels and a skirt tight enough to cut her stride in half. "Just a few reminders before you leave the building. All information pertaining to the future will be restricted on a need-to-know basis by your Praetorian--"

"You don't say," Adam mumbled under his breath.

"--and you'll be required to undergo another week of isolation before your return trip. Other than that, please give us a call if you need anything," she said, flicking a business card in his direction. "Especially in the case of any symptoms of time sickness."

Adam's gaze darted up from her card. "I have a question about that." He glanced back at Bruner, whose face was, as always, inscrutable. "The information packet EE supplied didn't specify the percentage of travelers that develop symptoms. It also failed to mentioned the long term effects were anyone to develop them."

Ms. Schneider frowned at him, as if not quite sure what to make of his question. She glanced at Bruner before saying, "The company felt those specifics weren't necessary for the average traveler to know, and the FDA agreed."

"Are you saying EE is refusing to share this information?"

Bruner placed a hand the size of a shovel blade on his back, steering him toward the rotating doors. "You'll be fine. Let's go."

Placed unceremoniously into one of the door's slots and rotated out onto the sidewalk, at first glance, Adam was a little disappointed in the future. The weather was slightly warmer, it being September instead of October. The sun still shone at a sharp angle, casting the street in a relief of shade. He turned and stared up at the building he'd just exited, the bold double E logo backed by several colorful, geometric designs connected by bold black lines was the same as in his time. But nothing was built entirely out of shiny chrome, no flying cars zipped past, and the people on the street were not dressed in outlandishly tight, or severely geometrical clothing.

As far as he could tell without his glasses, the buildings surrounding him were the same. The cell phone provider across the street in 2016 was now some kind of virtual reality/video game experience. The building directly to the right, a restaurant advertising an African ethnic food he was unfamiliar with. Upon further scrutiny, there was far less green and open sky--not that there had been all that much in LA in his time. New construction had been squeezed into the already crowded street sometime in the last few decades, and several existing buildings now sported extra stories that looked like apartments.

A car whispered up to the curb. Adam marveled at the nearly silent engine, clearly electric. No surprise there. The car was sleek, making the ones from his era look like the aging chubby uncle next to the high school quarterback. Bruner ushered him into the back of the car, where Adam experienced his first legitimate futuristic double take. In the front seat was room for two or three more passengers… and that was it. No driver, no steering wheel or pedals, just a display for climate control and an television that took up the entire dash.

The car shot into the stream of traffic, and Adam instinctively pawed the air in alarm at being in a driverless vehicle.

Bruner's dry laugh echoed in the spacious backseat. "Don't tell me you're surprised at this? The first prototypes of this particular vehicle are being test driven as we speak back in your time."

"There's a big difference between an actual person sitting behind the steering wheel of a quote unquote 'self-driving' car and getting in what is the equivalent of a roller coaster minus the track," Adam said behind clenched teeth.

The car took a corner at what Adam considered a speed that would surely roll them, but he felt a pneumatic system kick into gear somewhere under his feet and compensate for the centripetal force. Their center of gravity corrected before it ever really was out of position, and they sailed around the corner without so much as a sway from the passengers in the back seat.

"Besides," Adam said as he inched away from the door, "there's obviously been a few upgrades since the prototype." The car next to them seemed to be centimeters away.

"Pretty remarkable," Bruner admitted, glancing around the back seat like he was marveling at the technology that made the first flushing toilet possible. "No one in an urban area owns cars anymore. Lane space is better utilized without having to have a buffer for human error, and optimal driving at all times has lessened commute time and traffic congestion."

"That's nothing short of a miracle for LA. Who knew traffic problems could be solved by taking humans out of the equation?" Adam said, mimicking Bruner's dry tone. "How does it know where to take us, anyway?"

"You can set the pickup and drop-off locations when you order the car," Bruner said, as the car glided to a quick and efficient stop in front of a set of wrought iron gates.

Chapter 3

Adam couldn't read the tiny white letters on the top of the gate, but it didn't matter. Greystone Mansion was an iconic landmark for anyone who grew up in LA, including Adam. He hadn't been here in years, but the grounds remained unchanged, probably not all that different than when it was built in the 1920's.

The mansion was a hive of activity. Caterers, florist,

half-dressed bridesmaids, and event rental employees swarmed the property that was the closest southern California came to the estates of Gatsby's world. Odd that Adam went fifty years into the future only to attend an event at a venue that took him to the distant past.

There were hints of the year 2070 here and there; hermetically sealed Plexiglas boxes to keep the live flowers as fresh as possible, tiny hearing aid type headsets or phones maybe that made everyone appear to be talking to themselves, and folding tables that seemed to spring into being with the touch of a button. Somethings were timeless though, the cut of the tuxedo the groomsmen wore, the ostentatious bridesmaid dresses, the frantic buzz that settled over everyone and everything involved with the wedding--including the woman at the gate. She was dressed in a suit just dark enough to be considered not white. With her tablet clutched to her chest like a lifeline and a guard dog type demeanor about the unfolding festivities, she could only be the wedding planner.

"Invitation?" she asked, already scanning the screen in her hands and not his face.

Adam extracted the invitation from his breast pocket and held it out as she rambled on.

"You're early. They won't be seating guests for another..." she trailed off when she finally noticed the invitation in his hand. She met his eyes with an expression that Adam couldn't name, but was unsettling just the same.

"Mr. Edelstein," she breathed without consulting her tablet. A smile lit her face, but her eyes didn't lose the strange look. Appreciation, Adam guessed. No, that wasn't quite right.

Adam gave her a hesitant smile in return. "Yes. How do you know my name?"

"Oh," the wedding planner looked flustered for a moment, but never lost her smile. "We only sent out two real invitations. Everything is digital these days, you know. Just couldn't figure out how to get an e-vite to the past..."

Her eyes roamed up and down Adam until he started to fidget.

"You know why I'm here, don't you?" Adam guessed. It had occurred to him, in fact he'd spent the better part of his week in isolation ruminating on it, that his future self might be here, somewhere. He'd only be seventy-five, after all. It was within the realm of possibility he was still around. But if so, why wasn't his future self presented with the invitation instead of him? It would have been a lot less trouble to get him there, unless...

Ms. Wedding Planner's gaze flickered over his shoulder, and Adam knew she was communicating something with Bruner, but he refused to look away, as if his determination alone could pry the information out of her.

"Of course I know," she replied, having come to some silent decision with Bruner.

"I'm dead, aren't I? I mean my future self." Adam had tried very hard not to examine this piece of reality too closely, tried to keep the mental image of his body lying in a dark grave somewhere at bay, but it was now staring him in the face.

"Of course not!" Ms. Wedding Planner gasped, and from the irritated noise Bruner made behind his head, Adam knew she had let something slip.

"That is to say," she said as she smoothed the front of her suit, trying to salvage her blunder, "your... benefactor is determined your attendance of the wedding... play out organically without any outside interference."

"My benefactor?" Adam whirled to face Bruner, but the Praetorian had enough of this woman's blundering. He escorted Adam past the stammering wedding planner and through the gates with an expression that should have turned anyone in his path to stone.

"What did she mean?" Adam demanded of his bodyguard. If anything, now he was even more confused.

"I'm afraid that's outside--" Bruner began to deadpan.

"Don't even say it," Adam growled, pushing past him into the mansion grounds. His irritated burst of anger didn't last long; he had no idea where he was going and the property was extensive.

Bruner seemed to sense his hesitation. "I believe the ceremony is in the formal gardens. If we wander a bit, we should be there as they began seating guests."

Adam nodded his assent, and that's how he ended up strolling the most romantic spot in Beverly Hills with his six-foot two bodyguard.

They wandered up the drive as Adam's mind drifted back to the sterile white room in the bowels of the Era Excursions building. Adam and Bruner followed the path to the front of the soaring stone mansion that was situated in the side of a cliff like a protrusion. While Adam's feet navigated the cobblestone courtyard, his mind was running through the possible mathematical scenarios that would explain how it was possible to artificially create the phenomenon of an x-point...

Bruner gave him a smug smile, like he knew exactly where his mind was. Perhaps Adam could talk him into a more thorough examination of the room before their return trip.

Following the path, they left the mansion and bustle of the wedding preparations far behind as they made their way further into the property. For the moment it was deserted, reinforcing the feeling of stepping back in time, not forward. So Adam was mildly surprised when two slim figures appeared from behind the decorative fountain at the end of the walk.

From this distance minus his glasses, Adam could only guess they were another pair of wandering wedding guests, passing time before the big event. He made to go around the fountain in the opposite direction, therefore avoiding any conversation with future individuals he didn't know and hopefully any awkward or embarrassing situations, but Bruner took that moment to suddenly take the lead, making a beeline for the couple. Adam grudgingly followed in his wake. When they reached them Bruner seemed disinclined to do anything but stand to the side and take in the view while Adam forced an uncomfortable smile.

This close to the women, he saw one lithe brunette with sepia-toned skin, clad in what Adam assumed was the height of fashion in 2070. Her dress was oddly shiny, severely corseted, and very angular. Her hair was cut in a short, uneven crop, and she was tall and muscled. Her face was an inscrutable mask of blank indifference in response to his attempted smile.

The other woman looked as uncomfortable and out of the place as Adam felt. She fidgeted with a lock of auburn hair that had come loose from her updo, constantly smoothing the front of a plain black cocktail dress, a color that seemed to make her hair glow in the dwindling light. The only other striking thing about her was an odd circular pendant of clear glass with dozens of colored dots suspended in it.

"Ladies," Adam said, tipping his head toward them in an awkward nod. Then casting around for something, anything to say to end the frosty glare on the brunette's face, and the lost look on the other's, "incredible place. Have either of you been here before?"

The brunette blinked, her gaze sliding away from Adam before she'd even spoke. "No."

"I have," the girl in the cocktail dress spoke up. "Not since I was a little girl, though. This place seems incapable of changing." She spun in a slow circle as she spoke, taking in the towering trees, the soaring gables of the mansion in the distance, and the sky, slowly being taken over by the hues of the setting sun.

"Me neither. The last time I was here was a sixth grade field trip."

"Me too! Did they make you play those old fashioned games in the formal gardens? Like Annie Over--"

"--and Kick the Can?" Adam finished with her. A smile tugged at his lips. He'd forgotten about that. Funny, they were still running those field trips this far into the future.

The girl in the cocktail dress seemed to relax slightly. She stuck her hand out at Adam as if on impulse. "Evelyn," she said and tilted her head toward her companion like an afterthought. "This is Zea."

Adam couldn't quite interpret her tone as she introduced the tall brunette, still studiously ignoring them all as she scanned the surrounding landscape. Not irritated, exactly, but certainly not friendly. He wondered what their relationship could be.

Evelyn was waiting with raised eyebrows, and Adam realized with a start he was still gripping her hand while his mind had drifted.

"Adam," he replied quickly, "and Bruner," he added, finally releasing her. He suddenly felt jumpy with his hands just dangling at his sides, so he stuffed them in his pockets. "Friend of the bride or groom?"

Evelyn darted a glance at Zea and seemed to tense up again. "We're--"

Strains of a string quartet playing light and sweet wandered over the hedge.

"Sounds like they're getting ready to start," Evelyn interrupted herself. She tilted her head at Adam. "Shall we?" They joined Zea and Bruner who had wandered to the far side of the fountain together and were speaking in low tones. They pulled apart as Adam and Evelyn approached, drifting behind them as they all made their way across the forecourt, with its sculpted hedges, symmetrically placed planters, and sweeping stone staircase.

Chapter 4

On the narrow lawn facing a towering Italian inspired fountain, hundreds of white chairs had been placed with military precision. A simple arch wound with white roses waited down the aisle for the bride and groom, reflecting the thousands of blooms bordering the garden.

Adam glanced down at Evelyn, who seemed to be drinking in the perfume of the roses almost cloying in their sweetness. She glanced up at him a small, embarrassed smile on her lips.

The usher caught sight of them and nearly bull rushed them in his eagerness.

"Un--I--um--Mr. Edelstein!" the usher gabbled. He was a younger, but tall. Adam had to crane his neck slightly to look the man in the eye. The usher goggled at Adam, his gaze sweeping up and down him like he couldn't quite believe what he was seeing. His scrutiny swung between Adam and Evelyn, a goofy smile taking over his face. The unease that had temporarily vanished the last few minutes in Evelyn's company came roaring back, and Adam glanced over his shoulder to catch Bruner's eye.

The Praetorian's blank gaze was, as usual, unhelpful, but there was something different about Bruner. Slightly less tension in his shoulders, a tiny hint of pleasure in his expression maybe.

"And Mrs.--um--Miss--" the usher stammered, a slightly panicked look in his eye.

"Newport," Evelyn supplied with a bemused smile and a sideways glance at Adam.

"Of course," the usher's relief was palatable. "Newport. I'd forgotten for a second."

He beamed at both of them with a smile so familiar, Adam wanted to squirm. He had the distinct impression these people knew him personally--well, the older him-- and had not just memorized his name off a guest list. Nice that they seemed to like him. Perhaps he was another distant relative?

"If you'll follow me?" the usher said, leading the way down the aisle and stopping second row from the front. Adam hesitated. Seats this far up were usually reserved for immediate family. He exchanged a glance with Evelyn who looked just as unsure, but they slid silently into their places, sandwiched between Bruner and Zea.

A few other guest had taken their seats, but the rest were sprinkled throughout the garden. The afternoon sun beat down, threatening to make Adam sweat in his rented tux coat, and the quartet in the corner of the garden continued to play a mild and romantic soundtrack to the event.

Adam stared at his hands as the minutes ticked by, and the chairs around them filled up. He hated this. Hated feeling out of place and not in control of the situation. Hated being in the dark. Hated feeling the social pressure to fill the silence with a complete stranger, no matter how pretty she was. This was exactly what he had been afraid of when he'd accepted the invitation.

And she was pretty. Adam had always had a thing for redheads, and his eyes kept drifting to the tendril of hair she wound round and round her thumb absently. Although he kept trying to regain his previous train of thought about time travel and quantum physics, having her this close wasn't making it easy.

She gave him an uncomfortable smile without meeting his eyes, and spoke more to the arch than him. "So, what do you do, Adam?"

"I'm a student."

Her caramel colored eyes found his, waiting.

"At MIT."

"Studying…" she asked with a roll of her hand.

"Physics. In particular, quantum mechanics…" Adam trailed off because Evelyn's face had taken on a beaming smile.

"Me too. Except I'm at Harvard and I haven't chosen my focus."

There was no way. Gorgeous and a physics major? What were the odds? Actually he knew the odds, and they weren't good.

"Astrophysics is more marketable these days," Evelyn continued to muse, "but quantum mechanics is just so…"

"…Fascinating," Evelyn said, finishing Adam's thought for him.

A goofy grin stretched across his face, and Adam quickly tried to reign it in. Evelyn's odd necklace caught Adam's eye again. This close, he could make out what it really was. The colored dots were actually tiny, complex geometrical shapes, connected by thin black lines creating a complicated, perfectly symmetrical pattern trapped in a piece of clear glass.

"Are you wearing an E8 necklace?" he asked.

The husky chuckle Evelyn gave him made Adam's heart soar.

"You are the *only* person to ever recognize it," she told him, clearly charmed.

"What kind of people do you hang out with, that they can't recognize the structure that underlies everything in our universe?"

Beside Adam, Bruner cleared his throat in poorly coded message that spelled out, *nerd.*

But Evelyn only seemed delighted. "You'd be amazed at who doesn't get it, even at Harvard."

This girl was way out of his league, in more ways than one. She lived in the *future* for Pete's sake.

"So are you a famous physics student from MIT? A lot of people here seem… interested in you," Evelyn said, glancing around surreptitiously.

Adam snorted a laugh. "Famous and physics student is an oxymoron."

But once she said it, he realized it was true. The garden was almost at capacity, and more than one head was turned in his direction, craning for a better view of their row, or whispering to their neighbor between glances at him.

"How do you know you're not the one they're staring at?" Adam asked, instantly kicking himself for not thinking

164

through the comment more thoroughly. Would she think he was hitting on her?

She raised one corner of her mouth in a crooked smile. "It's not my name the usher knew."

"Still, you're the better looking one."

On the other side of Evelyn he caught a less-than-amused look on Zea's face followed by an eye roll at his corny line. Adam pinched his lips shut. What was wrong with him today? If Evelyn didn't think he was flirting earlier, she certainly did now.

Evelyn's lips parted, her eyes full of amusement, but Adam never learned what her comeback would have been. At that moment, the string quartet struck up the music synonymous with weddings. Nice to know Pachelbel's Canon in D was as overused fifty years into the future as it was in Adam's time.

A man with a white collar and a nervous groom in formal wear materialized under the archway. The congregation rose and swiveled as one, each trying to catch the first glimpse of the bride. Beside him, Evelyn was practically in Zea's lap trying to see down the aisle. Bridesmaids paraded past, some tilting unsteadily on spiky heels, others creeping nervously between the rows of chairs, and one woman who must have been imaging a fashion runway the way she strutted past dragging her poor groomsman with her.

Pleased murmurs started at the back of the garden and rippled toward Adam as the bride made her way through the throng of people. She was nearly parallel to his seat before he could see her, clutching an older man's arm, beaming at one of the tux clad swains under the arch. Her burgundy hair caught his eye, as well as the way her gown seemed to glow in the gathering dusk; then she was past him, being handed off to the groom, and Adam ended up staring at the back of the wedding party's heads for the rest of the ceremony, which honestly, he mostly tuned out.

From the bits and pieces that washed over him,

weddings in 2070 weren't all that different from 2016. Not that he was an expert on matrimony or anything. However, there was an odd bit where he could have sworn the minister said, "Until cryonics do you part." And at one part of the ceremony the bride took clusters of small white flowers out of her bouquet and solemnly passed them to her bridesmaids, who happily tucked them in their own flower arrangements. The symbolism was lost on Adam.

There were kisses and applause, tissues dabbed eyes of the older women in the audience, which Adam only thought happened in sappy romantic comedies. The Wedding March played, the bride and groom clutched hands as they skimmed down the aisle, the audience seemed to give one happy prolonged sigh, and it was over.

Evelyn turned to Adam, beaming, not a trace of tears on her own cheeks. Everyone around them groaned as they got to their feet to begin their search for the free food and booze.

"You're staying for the reception?" she asked.

"I've got all the time in the world," Adam replied quite honestly. No matter how long he stayed in the future, he would return the same minute he had left. The burning desire to get back and examine the time machine didn't seem quite so urgent at the moment.

"Roo?" a gruff voice behind him called. Adam started at the name, then stiffened. The voice wasn't familiar, but who in the world would know that name here?

He turned, Bruner instantly at his side.

A stooped old man studied him over a hawkish nose, his dull gray eyes lighting with recognition immediately. "It is you! The family rumor mill said you'd be here, or at least, this version of you."

As he spoke his droopy neck skin flapped with each word. Adam had no idea who he was, or why he knew the embarrassing nickname he'd forbid his mother from using when he was thirteen.

Confusion must have been stamped on Adam's face.

The man barked out a laugh, "Of course you wouldn't recognize me, you lucky bastard!" and punctuated the curse with a surprisingly solid punch to Adam's bicep.

A memory snapped to the front of his brain like a wet towel in a boy's locker room, and Adam gasped as he recognized the person behind the layers of wrinkles. "Charlie?"

The old man's laugh morphed into a wheeze, but Charlie looked no less pleased to see Adam as he hacked into his fist for a moment. "Caught on faster than I thought, Roo!"

Adam rubbed his shoulder, more out of habit than anything. A punch was how Charlie had always said, "Hey you." Nothing expresses the joy of seeing your cousin like the bruise his knuckles left the next day.

"Charlie," Adam repeated, still trying to reconcile the teenage boy he'd seen last month at Thanksgiving with this squinty-eyed, denture wearer.

"Don't go looking at me like that," Charlie warned, waving a finger good naturedly under Adam's nose. "You look even worse than me. Every extra year wears like ten once you hit seventy." The end of this sentence was punctuated by another round of hacks and wheezes, giving Adam time to gather a coherent thought.

"If you're here, then it is a family wedding." He narrowed his eyes at his cousin. "You must know how I'm related. Why was the past me invited and not the present one?"

Charlie's knowing grin was the same one he'd given Adam fifty years in the past when he'd heard Adam's latest girlfriend had dumped him.

Bruner stiffened next to Adam, ready to intervene if Charlie tempted the fate of the world by divulging too much future information, but his cousin's gaze flicked over his shoulder briefly before shrugging and saying, "You'll figure it out before too long. See you on the dance floor!"

Charlie shuffled off, leaving Adam sinking deeper into

his swamp of frustration. Curious as to what had caught Charlie's interest behind him, Adam turned to find a mostly empty garden nearly leached of all daylight. The only people in view anymore were Evelyn and Zea, nearly out of sight themselves, trailing behind the rest of the guests to the reception.

"Ready?" Bruner asked in his deadpan style. Adam had to grin at his completely characteristic lack of words. But now that Evelyn's wide smile wasn't trained on him from a foot away, his thoughts turned again to the stark white room under EE headquarters.

One of his hands massaged his thumb, making the joint pop as Adam hedged, "Actually, I was thinking--"

"Of dancing, obviously," Burner said, placing a hand the size of a Christmas ham on his neck and steering him gently, if firmly, back to the entrance to the garden. The thump of celebration echoed down the cyprus walk, with the anticipation of intoxication so thick, it could almost form a tangible person to greet them at the entrance to the inner courtyard.

The courtyard was striking enough on an ordinary day, but tonight it had been transformed. One of several ostentatious fountains sprinkled around the mansion grounds was parked in the middle of the gray stoned enclosure. A white-tux clad orchestra was tucked into one of the stone arches tuning their instruments, and in the evening shadows vines bloomed with pinwheel-shaped white flowers creeping across the walls. The blooms were so thick the courtyard seemed to glow in the moonlight, casting an ethereal air over the festivities.

Adam nudged a blossom with a finger, only to have it pass straight through. The projection rippled, releasing a small shower of sparks that coalesced, forming a tiny winged creature. The firefly gave a realistic hum before bobbing over the linen draped tables dotting the courtyard.

"That is unreal," Adam said, turning in a slow circle as he took in the infusion of flowers and winking lights hovering over the scene.

"Cheaper than real flowers, too," Bruner added, killing Adam's bewitched mood.

Chapter 5

Bruner seemed to know right where their table was. When they drew close enough to compensate for Adam's lack of glasses, he recognized Evelyn's slim figure occupying one of the chairs, and he ridiculed himself for the way his heart stuttered for half a beat when he recognized her.

Her lips formed a full-wattage smile when she caught sight of him, which made up for the fact that Zea, still glued to her side, seemed to furrow her brow at him.

"Oh, good, familiar faces. I thought I'd be making small talk to strangers all night," Evelyn said, smoothing her dress down her thighs in a casual way that made Adam think she had no idea what the gesture was doing to the higher functions of his brain.

"You make fast friends," Adam said.

"Not usually," Evelyn said, glancing at her lap. She caught his gaze with a mischievous glint in her eye. "But anyone who recognized E8 has to be a kindred spirit."

A smattering of applause echoed as Adam turned to see the bride and groom step into the courtyard. They both gave shy little waves, making their way to the table for two set up in the middle of the melee. As if their arrival was a silent signal, waiters immediately began to circulate, placing tiny, pristine plates in front of guests.

"Caviar tartare," one whispered with reverence, floating Adam's first course in front of him without so much as a thump of the plate. Adam eyed the palm-sized minced raw meat with trepidation. A mound of tiny black spheres and slivers of green herb graced the top with artfully placed dabs of some kind of yellow sauce.

"If you squint and tilt your head, you can almost make out a face," Adam commented to his plate. Next to him

Evelyn let out an unladylike snort of laughter she quickly stifled. She picked up her silverware and took a careful forkful of the peculiar dish.

"One of the bridesmaids told me they hired the chef from the famous *Le Bernardin* in New York at great expense," Evelyn responded, taking a miniscule bite.

"Mmmm," Adam said noncommittally, picking up his fork like he might regret it. Next to him, Bruner was polishing off his own child-sized portion and sighing in contentment. Evelyn's eyebrows lifted in surprise as her own fork touched her tongue, immediately going in for a second bite. Adam gave in and took a taste for himself. If you could get past the I-shouldn't-be-putting-this-in-my-mouth texture, and the fact it was raw meat topped with fish eggs, it *was* good. Two bites in, he passed his plate to Bruner, who accepted it gratefully and made short work of it.

"Not your favorite?" Evelyn said with sympathy.

"I'm just hung up on Fat Sal's Fat Jerry sandwich," Adam said. He immediately mentally thumped himself. She wasn't going to have any idea what he was talking about.

"Doesn't hold a candle to his Pepperoni Pizza Burger," she countered, her smile widening as Adam realized he had a gobsmacked look on his face.

"I didn't realize you were from LA," he said, trying to downplay his stunned expression.

"Born and raised," Evelyn agreed.

The weird part of Adam was relieved to know he could still get a sandwich at Fat Sal's fifty years into the future. He probably shouldn't be, that place was a heart attack waiting to happen.

"Favorite beach?" Evelyn asked, snagging the glass of champagne Adam hadn't even noticed a waiter put in front of each of them.

"Easy, Venice."

Evelyn wrinkled her nose in response. "Too crowded. You can't beat Carrillo."

"It takes forever to get to Carillo," Adam argued, twirling the stem of his glass. "Football team? And don't you dare say the Rams."

"Never. My family bleeds Charger blue and gold."

"That was a close one. I thought I was going to have to switch tables."

"My turn. Elementary school?"

"One oh seventh," Adam announced, not liking the way Evelyn's easy, open smile vanished. "You?"

"Not important. Worst thing about LA?"

"You're not getting away that easily. Where'd you go to school?"

Evelyn sighed and all but mumbled, "Notre Dame."

Adam laughed, and swigged his champagne. "That hoity-toity private academy? No wonder you didn't want to own it."

"The fact that you got into MIT--"

"Coming from a destitute public school?"

"That's not what I meant. You got in on brains and hard work alone, and no one will ever question that."

Adam shrugged and glanced at the artfully arranged jumbo prawns and some kind of pureed vegetables that had appeared in front of him. "It's not a big deal. The one oh seven was a long time ago. By the time I was in high school, we had moved to Long Beach and I was lucky enough to attend the Academy." He glanced up and caught Evelyn's eye, "I mean, it'll never compare to *private* school, but still…"

She nudged his shoulder and grinned. "The traffic."

"What?"

"What I hate about LA. Can't stand being stuck in traffic."

"The ridiculous amount of sunshine," Adam countered, "and the traffic too."

His champagne glass was now empty, transferring the bubbles to his head. He relaxed into the floaty feeling, finding himself much more charming and personable than usual.

At the bride and groom's table, the couple rose, the bride's auburn hair catching the glints of the swirling fireflies, while her glowing dress making her look spectral. The groom led her to a nearby table with a towering, tablecloth-covered object.

"Ladies and gentlemen." The head waiter appeared next to the couple, his voice magically amplified like the excited whisper of a golf announcer. "The cutting of the cake."

With matching grins, the bride and groom hauled on a rope that hoisted the sheet up, revealing a tiered tower of white confection. While the precision of the four foot pastry would have put any architect to shame, Adam had just enough time to register how devoid of decoration it was before the courtyard was plunged into complete darkness. Adam swore he could feel his pupils dilating, but they instantly rebelled when the cake flamed to life and the orchestra struck a hard cord. The same vines and moon-drunk flowers that had adorned the walls of the courtyard now crept up the cake, twinning themselves together in time to the music until their pattern became clear.

"Julie Ann and Miles," Evelyn mumbled in the dark beside him, able to read the names at the same time.

This was followed by a five minute video of the couple's courtship, not unlike slide shows that Adam had seen at other weddings, but all curling around the cake in such clear 3-D, he itched to run a finger through it, just like the flowers made of light.

Just when he thought his senses were about to overload, the cake bust into dazzling jets of light and shot into the empty night above the courtyard, bathing the newly married couple in a fireworks finale that would have put any Fourth of July to shame.

"Whoa," Evelyn said beside him. "That was the cutting of the cake?"

Adam tried to blink the halo of light from his eyes.

The inconspicuous waiters had gone through the gathering again, depositing on their table some kind of brandied cherries. The sweet, spicy aroma smelled of decadence and wealth.

"Where's the cake?" Adam asked.

"No one *eats* cake anymore," Zea scoffed, moving aside the mound of cream in her bowl to get at the cherries. Adam blinked at the woman. He hadn't heard her say two words all afternoon.

"It's become more ceremonial," Bruner said, eyeing Adam's dessert. But Adam wasn't about to give away anything that had been soaked in alcohol.

"And now," the head waiter with his intense murmur was back, "the first dance." He bowed with a flourish, and Miles--Adam had to remember to call him Miles, not 'the groom'--swept Julie Ann onto the dance floor. At least he tried to sweep. He was so tense, heaved may have been more accurate. But Julie Ann was one of those naturally graceful human beings, and as the opening bars of an unfamiliar love song with an intense violin part played, the couple seemed to forget about the hundreds of people swooning into their brandied cherries and second glasses of champagne as they danced.

Adam had an excellent table, close enough to the dance floor to see the action without feeling like he was in the spotlight. The first dance ended to a smattering of applause and catcalls. The groom paired up with his mother, waddling her around the dance floor while guest dabbed at their eyes. By the time Julie Ann came back out with the same gray-haired gentleman whose arm she had hung onto while going down the aisle, Adam had mostly stopped paying attention.

The music, the dancers, and the shadowed guests on the side of the dance floor were all just background noise as the bubbles from his second--or was it his third?--glass of sparkling wine threatened to go up his nose. He was running an appreciative, and what he thought was a subtle, eye over Evelyn's marvelous silhouette when an inviting hand with an upturned palm appeared in his field of vision.

His gaze flew up the length of the arm, and he found himself staring at Julie Ann Julian's--no Rutherford's--beaming face.

"Finish the dance with me?"

Adam's hand seemed to meet hers of its own volition, his head getting in on the game as it bobbed an unsteady nod. He caught a brief glimpse of Evelyn's startled gaze and Bruner's furious one--not that you could tell by looking at him, but a week in quarantine with the man had taught Adam to look for the telltale clenching of the jaw and tick in the right temple.

Once Adam climbed to his feet, his woozy brain started to process the alarmed messages of 'what is going on?' coupled with 'this is not a good idea,' banging around his skull.

The bride seemed unconcerned with his lack of coordination, or the shell-shocked look his face, as they danced. Julie Anne watched his eyes closely, until Adam had to look away. She looked like she'd been trying to find something there.

"Your Praetorian looks like he just bit into a gooseberry," she whispered to him with a tiny laugh. "I knew he'd be furious, but I wasn't going to just avoid you all night." She peered into his face with another beaming smile. The color of her eyes looked familiar, a startling blue he knew he'd seen somewhere before. "Have you figured out who I am?"

"We're related somehow," he shrugged the shoulder she had her hand laid on. "But even that is just from a reasonable amount of context clues. No one will tell me anything."

"That's because the very thing they all hold dear has been threatened if they let anything slip."

"Their children?" Adam blurted out, alarmed.

Julie Ann's gasping laugh echoed around the courtyard. "No! The money."

This conversation was clearing up nothing for Adam. "What money?"

Julie Ann's grin widened as she dodged the question. "All I really wanted to say is I'm so glad you're here. It's been wonderful to see you, especially like this."

"Like what?" Adam actually glanced down at his chest before his brain slogged through the alcohol suspending his normally destitute social skills. "Oh, young, I suppose."

"And naive," she teased. "I can't wait to remind you that you didn't always know everything."

The tone of the song suggested it was winding down, as was their dance. Julie Ann glanced once more at their table where Bruner was watching them with his subtle death glare, Zea was running a bored finger around the rim of her water glass, and Evelyn was watching them with a bemused look on her face. "She seems lovely."

"Don't you know her?"

Julie Ann gave him a mysterious smile and a small curtsey, which Adam tried to reciprocate in the form of a bow, feeling like an idiot. She gave him a brief kiss on the cheek in a way that suggested the gesture was habitual for her. She glided over to Miles, waiting on the side of the dance floor with a patient smile. The newlyweds clasped hands as Adam stumbled back to his table where Evelyn and Zea had disappeared.

Chapter 6

"What did she say to you?" Bruner accosted Adam as he sank back into his seat, groping for his water glass.

"Nothing to get your Praetorian blood all fired up," Adam said, gulping half the glass in one go and sighing in relief. "She just wanted to thank me for coming."

"That's it?" Bruner asked, his gaze darting between Adam and Julie Ann, who was making rounds to each table with Miles in tow.

"She was as enigmatic as the rest of you."

Bruner smoothed the front of his tux. "Fine. But no more wandering off."

Adam rolled his eyes in a little-used gesture leftover from his teenage years. "I was in your line of sight the whole time."

"Good." Bruner straightened his tux again, his eyes darting through the darkness somewhere behind Adam's head. If he didn't know any better, Bruner looked almost... nervous. He was acting strange, that was for sure. Well, stranger than normal.

"Now, if you'll excuse me, it's time for a dance." He extended this open palm into the dark of the courtyard, and seemed to pull Zea from some kind of void behind Adam. The silent way that woman moved was spooky.

"Where's Evelyn?" Adam asked.

"Powder room," Zea replied, not even looking at him. "She'll be right back."

With their linked hands, Bruner raised his arm in a silent command, and Zea spun onto the dance floor into his embrace. They joined other couples waltzing to a song from the bygone big band era.

"Does it seem like they know each other?" Evelyn asked from the shadows. Adam had never realized how easy he was to sneak up on without his glasses.

"So it's not just me," Adam said, watching as Bruner dipped Zea so low her hair brushed the floor. The Praetorian's face remained inscrutable.

"I tried to ask Zea, but she didn't answer me."

Adam snorted. "I didn't even bother asking Bruner."

Evelyn had come to stand behind Adam to watch the dancers. While his eyes were trained on the other couples, he wasn't really seeing them. All of his other senses were going into overdrive with Evelyn this close. The faint lavender scent drifting off of her, her nearly inaudible breath, the warmth her skin seemed to radiate...

"Would you like to dance?" Adam was rather proud of how steady his voice came out.

He could feel Evelyn smile behind him. "How about a walk instead?"

Adam almost sagged with relief. Trying to waltz, especially on the same dance floor as Bruner and Zea, would have only ended in humiliation.

They slipped out of the courtyard, grinning like teenagers skipping class. They needn't have worried, Adam's minder never looked up.

Slightly breathless from their escape, and in Adam's case from his lack of any regular cardio, they sank back against the cool stone of a nearby wall. Evelyn laughed softly, her gaze finding Adam's in the dark, silent happiness in her expression. She tilted her head back and Adam followed her line of sight to the sky. His breath left him in one prolonged exhale. Beside him, Evelyn nodded in silent agreement.

"I've never seen so many stars," Adam whispered. "I guess the light pollution got better with the traffic."

"I may have lied earlier," Evelyn said, glancing down and twiddling her purse straps.

"Uh-oh. Is this where you tell me you're really a man, or we're secretly related?"

She laughed. Adam would happily work every day for the rest of his life to hear that laugh on a regular basis.

"Let's hope not." Her gaze returned to the sky. "No. I think I *have* made up my mind about my major. I'm just too chicken to admit it to myself."

"Ah," Adam nodded his head sagely, unable to tear his eyes away from the heavens. "Well, the astrophysics win another one. Although I do see the attraction."

The last sentence was directed not at the heavens, but at Evelyn, in an uncharacteristic ballsy move on Adam's part, probably partially fueled by the dwindling buzz of champagne.

She grinned to acknowledge the terrible pick-up line,

but didn't move her gaze from the sky, reciting: "Many people feel small, because they're small and the Universe is big. But I feel big, because my atoms came from those stars."

"Oh, no," Adam groaned and hung his elbows on his tented knees. "Is that that corny Michio Kaku quote?"

"You started it," Evelyn said, poking him in the side. "I do see the attraction? Please."

Adam gave a mock sigh and stood, offering his hand to Evelyn. "A guy's gotta try."

Evelyn didn't answer, but cocked one eyebrow very Bruner-like and took his hand. He helped her to her feet and they continued to wander the grounds of Greystone. Under a bright gibbous moon and the heavenly bodies that fascinated Evelyn so much, it did not escape Adam's notice that her warm, slender fingers stayed tucked into his.

They strolled further from the party, the strains of the band nearly swallowed by the night. Eventually the wrought iron and glass doors of the mansion's main entrance blocked their path. Adam put both hands up to shade his eyes and tried to peer in.

"Think it's open?"

Evelyn smoothly pulled open the door and glided past him with a coy, "I think so."

The interior was dark and silent. Even so, the vaulted drop ceiling tiles, the triple cathedral windows leading to the terrace, and the archways that mirrored them in the dim moonlight were electrifying. Evelyn led the way, and Adam was all too happy to observe her figure from behind as she eased a hand down the intricately worked wooden banister, her heels clicking on the marble steps as she descended under the suspended chandler to the grand entry way. Adam could picture her here, flapper dress swinging, part of the distant past the house belonged to.

Adam shook the vision from his head and followed her down the stairs.

"What a marvelous dance floor," Evelyn said turning a slow pirouette.

"Low coefficient of friction," Adam commented, immediately wanting to palm himself in the forehead.

Evelyn just turned up the wattage on her smile as she said, "You want to come and try it out for yourself, Mr. Newton?"

Adam stepped off the bottom step to join her, toeing the black and white alternating tiles. "Reminds me more of a chess board."

"Of course it would," Evelyn said with wry smile. "Are you any good?"

Adam shrugged one shoulder. "Depends on who I'm playing."

"All right." Evelyn paced back a few steps, taking careful measurements with her eyes. "We've got enough squares. All we need are pieces."

There was no way she was serious.

Thumbing open the clasp to her handbag she dug around for a second before flourishing a small cylindrical object at him. "My queen." She placed it on the floor at her feet, and only by squinting could Adam make out a tube of lipstick.

She was serious.

Adam glanced around before appropriating a vase from a nearby windowsill and setting it in the corresponding square. The next five minutes were a mad dash for chess pieces. Evelyn was at an advantage with the contents of her purse at her disposal, but Adam managed to cobble together eight pawns by removing the roses from the vase and setting them in an orderly line. His king was a potted plant, a pair of knights matching curtain ties, the stanchions meant to keep them out of this space made excellent rooks, and he sacrificed his cuff links to play bishops.

Evelyn's side of the board was even more bizarre, if smaller, including the heels off her feet, two abandoned champagne flutes; and compliments of the purse, a pair of cheap 3-D glasses and six perfect origami swans.

Adam lost spectacularly. He was amazed at how little he cared. It seemed much more important to watch the way Evelyn fiddled with her E8 necklace when she was thinking, or the tiny huffs of satisfaction she made when she removed one of his captured pieces from the board.

In five moves he realized he was outgunned. In fifteen, she had him in checkmate; although to be fair, he lost one of his bishops for a few turns because he couldn't find his tiny cufflink in the dark on the black tile. It was also ridiculously easy for her to slip her queen past him when it was so small and the moon their only source of light. A point he made sure to make.

Her only response, "All's fair in love and lipstick," was accompanied by a smirk as she snapped her purse shut again.

What happened next was so uncharacteristic for Adam, he felt like he was watching himself from a great distance. He observed himself twining his fingers around Evelyn's free hand, gently tugging her toward him until the space between their bodies disappeared. The pulses in their throats seeming to beat in time. Gathering her against him with an arm tight along her waist, he bent his lips to hers.

Adam suddenly seemed to snap back into his body which felt... as if it were made up of the same stuff as the stars. Maybe Michio Kaku wasn't so corny after all.

Chapter 7

Lost as he was in Evelyn, it took not one, but two alarming sounds to cut through his preoccupation. The meaty smack of a fist on someone's vulnerable body part didn't bring him around, but seconds later the crash of glass directly at his back did.

Tucking Evelyn behind him with a protective instinct he didn't know he possessed, Adam spun to see Bruner on the terrace, calmly choking the life out of a man. His neck was squeezed into the crook of Bruner's beefy bicep, his limbs windmilling desperately, all while his face took on the color of an eggplant.

The fight finally left the man with his last breath, and Bruner laid him gently on the floor, clear of the shattered glass, and checked his pulse.

"What... what..." Adam gasped at the Praetorian, unable to get his brain to process past that one word.

"Only found one shooter, but I'm assuming there are more," Zea announced, crunching across the terrace through the now empty window pane. "We need to move."

One tight nod from Bruner was all he got before the man had his arm in a vice-like grip. Zea manhandled Evelyn in a similar one. Bruner shoved Adam out the shattered window onto the terrace while Zea dragged Evelyn toward the side kitchen exit.

Adam put on the brakes. At least he tried. It was like trying to slow down a two thousand pound draft horse. "Wait! I'm not leaving her."

"Adam!" Evelyn called after him.

Bruner didn't slow, but he did give Adam motivation for moving in a tight, clipped voice. "It's safer for her. It's you they want."

Across the room, Zea was murmuring in Evelyn's ear as she pulled her in the opposite direction. Adam caught Evelyn's gaze one last time, her look of fear blended with a trace of regret and a watery smile, before she disappeared down the hall.

"What's going on?" Adam gasped as Bruner all but tucked him under his arm and took off. They ran across the terrace, down the cliff face by a set of stone steps, and across the lawn dotted with pine trees. Adam stumbled through the night, nearly blind in the dark, unfamiliar terrain.

His question was ignored, but Bruner did start talking

to himself. "South side. Service gate. Thirty seconds."

It wasn't until he tapped his ear that Adam realized Bruner was wearing some kind of high tech phone.

At Doheney Road, a car was waiting for them, identical to the one that had dropped them off hours earlier. Bruner shoved Adam in, sliding in behind him, and the car rolled forward with a terse, "Go," from the Praetorian.

Bruner never relaxed, his eyes darting through the tinted windows to the darkened, sparsely driven streets they were zipping through.

The shaking started soon after, and the harder Adam tried to control his trembling, the more violent it became.

"Put your head between your legs," Bruner said, gently guiding Adam into the correct position. "Take deep breaths. Slow and even."

It took at least a minute of staring at the floorboard and struggling to fill his lungs before Adam could gasp out, "What. Is. Going. On?" with more vehemence than he thought he was capable of with so little breath.

Bruner's eyes never left off scanning the streets, but his voice, gentler than Adam had ever heard it, addressed him nevertheless. "Did you ever wonder about the person who created time travel?"

The trembling of Adam's limbs had abated some, but he squeezed his eyes closed in defeat. Even a near-death experience hadn't earned him a straight answer from Bruner. Adam didn't have the energy for this game.

It didn't seem to matter, Bruner barreled ahead with his monologue. "Of course you have. Besides the fact that it's one of your time's--and this time's--great mysteries, you're... you." The last word didn't seem to need any further explanation as far as Bruner was concerned. "You have to realize a man like that... well, people are going to want what's in his head." Bruner's eyes flitted to Adam's hunched over form, as if to check he were listening. "But what most people don't realize was that it wasn't one man's genius. Or even two that created time travel. It was

182

a couple. A husband and wife."

Burner seemed to smile inwardly. "Of course, he got most of the credit, a fact he--to this day--hates, but they decided it was safer if she was seen as an unassuming wife and not the world's most brilliant astrophysicist."

Grunting in Bruner's direction to let him know that he'd heard him, but still wasn't happy about his lack of cooperation, Adam tried raising his head a fraction of an inch.

Bruner glanced at him before returning to his constant street scanning. "Almost there. Anyway, the husband got the last laugh. He insisted on naming the company after her."

"What, was her name Era? Excursions? How would you shorten that? Cursi?" Adam said, his breathing recovered enough to be sarcastic.

Shaking his head as if dissuading a serious thought, Bruner replied, "No, that name got used just because it matched her initials. Here," Bruner thrust a scrap of paper at Adam. He could just make out an unfamiliar phone number. "She would have given it to you if she'd had the chance." He fixed Adam with a much more Bruner-like stare than this nearly nostalgic person who'd body snatched him during the car ride. "Don't screw it up this time."

The car slowed to a stop and Bruner got out to open Adam's door. He climbed from the car on untrustworthy legs. They had pulled into a dimly lit parking garage next to an unassuming steel door that had the Era Excursions logo over it. Some kind of underground entrance then. Why wasn't he surprised? Right back where he started.

The significance of the number in his hand finally processed in the only part of his brain that was ever sluggish, the all-important social cortex. "This is Evelyn's?" He shook his head part in exasperation and part in disgust. "What good is this going to do me? I can't dial the future."

"Who said she's from this time?" Bruner said, pulling open the steel door for him with an amused expression.

Adam glanced at the Praetorian's face, narrowing his eyes at him while his brain ran back through his evening with Evelyn.

Her vague answer to who she knew at the wedding.

Zea, who seemed to know Bruner and not Evelyn.

Her field trip in sixth grade.

The entire wedding guests list looking at them with tightly sealed lips and knowing grins.

Bruner setting them up, *letting* them wander off...

Oh.

"Bruner," Adam asked in a quiet voice. "Is Fat Sal's still open?"

"Closed down over twenty years ago." There was that damned eyebrow again. Adam hadn't seen it in hours. "You were heartbroken."

Adam glanced back at the Era Excursions sign, his mind buzzing, trying to find the right slots for the puzzle in his head. If he could just find the puzzle the pieces went to.

The odd geometric shapes on the sign suddenly came into focus and imposed themselves on an odd necklace in Adam's recent memory--one of a kind really--that the wearer liked to flip around when thinking...

"Is that--that," Adam pointed a finger that had begun to shake again at the logo, as Bruner ushered him into a familiarly depressing, sterile, white hallway, complete with an expressionless Praetorian in an impeccable black suit.

"Now, Mr. Edelstein, go on with Cyrus. He'll get you home in one piece."

"You're not coming?" Adam asked, feeling a pang of loss an hour ago he would have snorted at if anyone were to suggest it.

"My journey was a return trip."

"What about the men with the guns?"

"They were never trying to kill you. Just capture you."

184

Bruner waved away this concern with a tone that suggested Adam was being a bit dramatic. "They don't even exist in your time. Once you're home, you'll be safe."

"Home," Adam said dumbly, allowing himself to be passed into Cyrus's care. But as he passed through the doorway, two of the floating puzzle pieces snapped together for Adam.

He turned back to Bruner. "Did you say 'this time?'"

"Sir?"

Adam shook his head at the Praetorian, determined to get a straight answer out of him. "You said, 'don't screw it up *this time*,' like I've..." A sick feeling lodged itself in Adam's midsection and oozed through the rest of his body. "Bruner, have I met Evelyn before?"

Instead of the inscrutable mask, for the first time, Adam could see the wheels turning in Bruner's head as he sorted through the possible answers and implications, finally landing on the one he could live with.

"Technically, no." Bruner's next words were strung together carefully, as if the fate of the world hung in the balance. "But something got... messed up and you've spent the majority of your life trying to set it straight." He gave Adam a wan smile. "Don't derail it now you're at the final stop. Your curiosity has always been your own worst enemy. Don't give in to it, just this once."

"Then how will I know the right thing to do?" Adam whispered. The fear he'd felt while being shot at was laughable to the terror coursing through him now.

"Where Evelyn's concerned? Always follow your gut."

Adam nodded slowly, biting back all his questions and doing his best to tune out his need for a full explanation.

Bruner nodded encouragingly as Cyrus led Adam the rest of the way into the building. "See you soon, sir."

Janna is a Colorado based YA author who loves a good fairy tale. Her works include the *Grimm Tales* series.

She's married to her own real life Prince Charming, and will usually admit to being mom of Joseph, Olivia, and the incorrigible middle child, Benny. Besides wrangling her kids, she can be found doing some therapeutic baking, dreaming of the ocean, and of course, curling up with a good book. Learn more at janna.patchwork-press.com

NOT SO ALONE
KELLIE BEAN

Two years ago, if you'd asked me where I saw myself living after graduation never in a million years would I have said New Hapsburry. Because no matter how you look at this place there's no getting around the fact that it is just so very... suburban.

Ugh.

This is not at all what I'd pictured for myself. For my life. Even a year before I'd finished up my business degree I would have told you I was headed for somewhere like New York, or Chicago, maybe even Portland. The stories I returned home with would be all about the different kinds of people I'd met, how I'd made the most of my public transit commute into the office, and my adventures exploring the city on the weekends.

But it turned out that those cities didn't want me quite as much as I'd wanted them. At least, none of the jobs I'd been able to get in any of those cities had been willing to pay me enough to actually live there.

If nothing else had come up maybe I would have considered working a second job on weekends or commuting two hours each way so I could live somewhere less expensive. But then I'd gotten a job offer from a small firm in New Hapsburry that paid well, offered great benefits, and was in a location where I could actually afford to have my own place without even needing a roommate.

It was almost too good to be true At least if I could ignore the fact that there really wasn't anything to do in this town.

For my first month after moving to the middle of New Hampshire for a job I didn't necessarily want, but desperately needed, I had ignored the emptiness that followed me everywhere. I'd thrown myself into my new job and had completely devoted myself to getting up to speed and being the best new paralegal that Holmes and Henderson had ever seen.

But there's only so long a person can go before they genuinely need a weekend off or, at the very least, need to mix up their routine enough so they don't go insane.

Which is what I'm trying to do now Sitting on a nearly empty bus and riding into the stretch of shops I keep hearing people refer to as Downtown Hapsburry. But this isn't my first trip, and where I'm heading there isn't anything remotely resembling a downtown area. But it's Sunday morning and I really couldn't spend another minute sitting around my apartment watching Netflix.

Looking back, I probably should have searched for a roommate, even if I didn't need one, just so I would have someone to talk to. But, I'm locked into a one year lease now, with no room for anyone else to move in without driving me crazy thanks to cramped quarters.

The bus pulls to a stop in front of one of New Hapsburry's three grocery stores and I exit through the backdoor. We're not quite all the way to the main section of town yet, but it's a nice day, and thanks to my new role as a cubicle drone I could use the exercise.

New Hapsburry is easily one of those places that can

be described as quaint. Walking just beyond the grocery store I come to a long row of townhouses, each one painted a different shade of blue, past that an antique store. Next to the store is a dentist's office that advertises that it has been family owned for fifty years.

It seems like everything in this place has existed for at least a century. Which doesn't exactly give me any hints about what I can do to pass the time on a Sunday morning. There are a few other people out on the street—an older man in a flat cap with a ketchup stain down the front of his shirt, a woman with her two small children—but no one more than glances at me as I pass by.

Maybe this was a mistake.

I could have stayed home this morning, and slept in, then drove into the city tonight. Things would probably be different if I'd managed to really get to know even just one person from work. If I had one person who would be up for exploring the town, and who would like to get brunch some time, I wouldn't feel so lonely. But so far, my new office has proved to be a little cliquey, and while everyone has been friendly enough, I still don't feel as though I've made any real connections. Every time I talk to my mom she promises it will happen naturally over time, but walking alone down the sidewalk on a beautiful day certainly makes me wish my life would get itself together already. I'm about to turn into a small coffee shop to settle in with a latte and a book for a little while when a building across the street catches my eye.

Morrow County Animal Shelter. Cat adoption fair, this weekend only.

Huh. I've never been a pet person because my parents never had pets while I was growing up, and in college, I barely managed to keep my houseplant alive. But maybe I can go inside just to interact with the cats and anything else they might have in there. I'm not sure it will entirely scratch my itch for some human interaction, but it definitely can't hurt. And if these guys are looking for homes, then maybe they'll appreciate the extra company as much as I do.

I only look back at the coffee shop once, still tempted to grab a caffeine fix, but my side trip to the shelter shouldn't take long. I can be in and out in a few minutes having done something at least a little interesting for the day. This will also give me something cute to add to my Facebook feed so no one at home looks too closely at how boring my new life is.

Traffic seems to be all but non-existent on this street right now, so I don't bother going to the crosswalk before sprinting across the road.

Beside the front entrance to the shelter is glass display case, looking right into a shaded enclosure housing three black cats. One suns itself up against the glass, while the other two snooze nearby, tangled up in one another. Past them, I can see a woman in blue scrubs moving around inside the front office. I move to the door only to find a closed sign hanging on the window.

Crap. So much for that idea.

But as I move back past the front window I find a smiling face waving me back toward the door. A black girl with thick, curly hair opens the main door to the shelter and ushers me inside. "We're not technically open yet, but since you're already here you might as well come inside," she says by way of a greeting.

"Are you sure?" I don't want to be any trouble, but at her inviting smile, I'm inclined to just go with it. If nothing else, it's nice to be seen.

"If you're here to look around and meet some of our pets, then you can do that as easily now as twenty minutes from now. I'm Tess, if you need anything."

"Thanks. I'm Erin." I have no idea why I bother to introduce myself. I should probably explain that I'm really only here because I needed something to do, but since she's already gone out of her way to be friendly, I keep quiet instead. I can always slip back out a little later when she's busy.

As soon as I'm through the very first doorway past the front office the space around me springs to life and is filled with barking and happy whines. Dogs of every size line kennels against both walls and as I continue down the corridor. I see everything from a white curly-haired dog with floppy ears to a shaggy black and white mutt along with more pitbulls and chihuahuas than I can count.

Every single dog responds as soon as it sees me, either by rushing to the front of the cage, tail-wagging, or retreating to a back corner. The whole thing is a little overwhelming, and leaving me to breathe a sigh of relief as soon as I'm through to the other side. When the door clicks shut behind me, it only muffles the noises instead of cutting them off completely, but it's enough to relax me.

I like dogs, and they seem to like me well enough, but I mostly seem to like them in three minute intervals when I meet a new one at a park or a friend's house.

Right away, I can tell that the cat room is far more my speed. But I can also see why it's the cats they're throwing the adoption fair for. While this room is probably smaller than the last one there have to be at least twice as many cats maybe more. Against one wall metal cages are stacked one on top of the other. The other side of the room is made up of three, bigger multi-level enclosures, each housing several felines.

I approach the first cage on my right and find yet another black cat staring back at me with unblinking yellow eyes. I try putting my hand out near the cage to see if he—the piece of paper attached to his cage declares he is in fact a male, named Kringle—responds, but the cat doesn't move.

Okay, next question. How do you make friends with cats? I leave Kringle to whatever he was up to before I interrupted him and crouch down to meet whoever lives underneath him. I come face to face with an orange tabby who looks so small; they can't possibly be full grown. His name is Walter and he's only six months old. My heart melts a little when he presses his body right up against the mesh door to his cage, and doesn't flinch when I stroke his fur through the small holes.

"Hi, Walter," I coo at him feeling a little silly as soon as the words leave my mouth. But Walter doesn't seem to mind in the slightest and purrs a happy response.

I sit there just scratching Walter and speaking pretty much nonsensically until someone else enters the room from behind me, reminding me where I am.

"Oh, Walter is a sweetie," Tess, the girl from earlier, says giving me a knowing look. "Have you ever had a cat before?"

I shake my head. "I didn't really come from a big pet family."

"Well, there's never a bad time to start. And I love that you're looking at adopting an older cat instead of getting a kitten for your first fur-baby."

I can't help but raise my eyebrows at the term fur-baby, but if Tess notices my reaction, she doesn't say anything.

"How many pets do you have?" I ask, mostly to change the subject. I'm half-expecting her to say something outrageous like seventeen.

Instead, Tess frowns. "None right now. I'm a student at the university, and dorm life means no pets. But at least I have this job, and I visit my parents and our dogs every month or two."

My fingers are still kneading into Walter's fur as Tess chatters on about the two dogs her parents have. I'm only startled away from listening to a story about a lab taking an impromptu dip in her parents' pool by a rumbling coming from inside the cage.

"He likes you," Tess says, as a second girl in scrubs enters the room from behind her, not giving us a second look. "But to be fair, Walter seems to like everyone. He's definitely a people cat. He's super friendly."

Tess stares at me expectantly, and I get the distinct

impression that she's expecting me to volunteer to take Walter home any second now. And now I feel like a pretty horrible person for getting her hopes up. But it's not like I can admit that I didn't come in here for the cat adoption fair today. I just came to... what? Distract myself?

But as I smile politely at Tess, I'm still secretly enjoying the feeling of Walter's scratchy fur under my fingers. Even just being near him makes me feel a little less lonely.

It's possible that I actually came in here for some company. And Walter has definitely delivered. Plus he seems to be enjoying having someone to hang out with as much as I am.

Tess's face falls a little when I don't respond to her. "Okay then. Well, I should get back to the front. Let me know if you need anything."

Maybe I didn't come to the shelter today looking to adopt a cat. But I'm definitely enjoying this cat's company. Is there any real reason why that needs to end right now? I need someone to spend time with when I'm at home. Especially since I don't exactly have an abundance of friends at work right now. Or even in this state. And Walter needs a home. It seems like a pretty good match to me. If not an entirely expected one.

"Wait," I say, a little too loudly right as Tess reaches the door that will take her out of the cat room. If she leaves I'll probably chicken out. Thankfully, she turns around and I breathe a sigh of relief. As unexpected as all of this is, it's something I want to do. Maybe even need to do. With just one word I changed my whole world, and all of a sudden, I feel lighter than I have since I first moved to New Hapsburry.

No longer than five minutes later I'm sitting in a cramped office at a desk across from Tess, who still has a broad grin plastered on her face, filling out an application that asks me all of the questions I'd expect, and a few that I absolutely didn't see coming—like my entire, typical weekly schedule. But I fill out each answer as best I can silently hoping that the answers I'm giving are the right ones.

Even though I didn't even know this was something I wanted when I woke up this morning I already know I'll be devastated if it doesn't work out. Walter is still back in his cage in the other room. If I'm rejected and never come back for him he'd never know the difference. But I'd know.

God, I want this so much, and I can't even explain it.

"So you're at work about ten hours a day?" Tess asks, reading over the paper I've handed to her after rereading each of my answers.

My teeth tug on the inside of my lip before I answer. "Including my commute back and forth, yeah. I don't have a car here yet." I almost don't want to ask this next part. "Is that a problem? I mean, if he's going to be too lonely or something..." What? What could I do? Ask my neighbors who I've barely spoken to if they can pop in and visit my cat during the day?

Tess shakes her head emphatically. "He'll be fine," she answers, her tone both calm and reassuring. "I was just thinking that since you hadn't picked up any supplies yet, we could look into free feeding him, rather than doing set meals every day, so you don't have to worry too much about your schedule."

A huff of air escapes from my chest in relief. She's being so nice about this, but it still feels like everything could go wrong at a moment's notice. I'd like to think that I would have spent weeks preparing for a day like today. That essentially adding a new member to my family isn't something I'd just do on a whim. But the reality is that this is pretty much par for the course for me... deciding something on a whim and then sitting back and hoping my world doesn't explode around me. Moving to a new state, most of my relationships, my major in university, and now

194

getting a cat—I'm kind of known for leaping first then thinking up all of the ways things can go wrong as I I plummet back down to Earth.

Tess doesn't say anything else, but her eyes continue to scan my application, as I sit rigid in the chair across from her with my fingers knotted together as I try to look like a responsible adult who can be trusted with the care of another life.

A clock ticks overhead and I think the silence might be killing me. "If there's anything I can do to make this a better fit for Walter, please just let me know," I say, stammering a little at the end. "I swear, I'll do everything I can to make sure he's happy and healthy. I'll find a regular vet and get him checked up right away, maybe look into cat play dates…"

Tess chuckles, cutting me off before I can ramble out any more ideas as they jump into my head. "You might be overthinking this a little. Getting a vet is a great first step. But taking a cat on play dates is definitely going to be more of a headache than anything, and honestly, I'm not sure he'll appreciate it. I promise, he'll be totally fine doing his own thing, and the two of you will fall into a routine before you know it."

Tess pauses, putting down the piece of paper on the desk in front of her before giving me a long look and continuing. "If you're that worried though, there might be another option for you…" At that she stares me down like I'm supposed to be able to figure out on my own exactly what she's thinking. Instead, I simply blink at her worried this is yet another test I'm not going to pass.

"Keep in mind that this is absolutely optional, but how would you feel about potentially adopting a second cat?"

My mouth drops open, only a little, but enough that Tess catches the expression. "Nevermind," she quickly amends. "I probably shouldn't have said that. Zero pressure from me. It was just an idea."

I'm getting the impression that by suggesting a second

cat, she's broken a rule of some kind. But I'm not put off by the suggestion, not even annoyed, mostly just surprised.

"With a second cat... they'd be able to keep each other company when I'm not around?" I guess.

I may be about to get in way over my head.

Half an hour later as the shelter starts to fill with people, I'm balancing myself between two cat carriers. I let Tess pick out my second companion for me since I'd basically picked my first cat at random anyway. All I'd asked for was one she was a fan of, who would get along with Walter, and who maybe wouldn't be so lucky in finding a home on his own today.

I ended up with another male cat, this one solid gray and nearly eight years old, who watched me—maybe even judged me—with wide, green eyes from his spot across from me on the bus as the three of us made our way home. His name was Simon, and Tess had assured me that he was a giant sweetheart, but that he needed some time to warm up to new people. So now I have two cats and next to no cat supplies. Apparently, they didn't need much, but I was still going to have to get myself some food and a litterbox if nothing else.

It takes an embarrassingly long time to unlock the door to my apartment and get the two crates inside. Especially since I'll be leaving again in only a minute to head back out to the pet store which thankfully seems to be in walking distance. The door closes behind me with a terrifying click as it dawns on me that I'm now alone with and solely responsible for two cats. My cats.

"I guess I'll let you guys out to stretch your legs while I'm gone," I say out loud, already feeling silly. "You live here now too, so you may as well get comfortable."

I set both crates down just outside the door to the kitchen for no reason other than it's the biggest stretch of available space in my small home. By the time I open the door to Walter's crate I'm holding my breath, but when the door swings open nothing happens. He just sits there staring at me.

"Fair enough," I mutter and move to open Simon's crate. As soon as the door is completely open and I've moved my hand away, he's on the move, faster than I would have thought he could move. I squeal a little and startle backward, but he's not coming for me. Instead, he takes off like a shot toward my bedroom running in what has to be a blind panic.

So, that didn't go well. And Walter still isn't doing much of anything. "Maybe I'll leave you guys alone for a while to settle in." I stand back up glad there wasn't anyone around to see me freak out at the first sign of life from my new pets.

"I'll be back soon," I promise as soon as I make it back to the front door, wondering if it'll be helpful to start getting them used to my voice. When I slip outside I double check to make sure the cats aren't attempting to follow me out toward freedom, but neither cat comes anywhere near me. They seem to want to stay as far away from me as possible. They can probably sense just how hopeless I am.

Still while Tess did promise that if things didn't work out, I could bring the cats back, no questions asked... I'm excited. I've got cats!

I'm back home within the hour already looking forward to seeing Walter and Simon again. It takes a bit of awkward maneuvering to get myself back through the front door without risking any escapes, but I make it work, now weighed down with a whole new slew of cat supplies. Thanks to my new job and a limited social life, I could afford to spend a little extra, and pick the food recommended by the woman working at the pet store, a litter box and litter, and as many toys and treats as I could fit inside the still empty litter box to carry the whole awkward setup back home. I probably would have grabbed a scratching post if I could have found a way to strap it to my back.

"I'm home," I call out.

I wasn't expecting the cats to come running, but from where I'm standing there's absolutely no sign of them. My place looks exactly like it has almost since the day I moved in.

A few more steps inside reveals the crates again near the door separating living room from kitchen, and now both are empty. Which I guess is a good sign.

Maybe? I have no idea.

"Do you guys want food?" I ask, putting everything down on the table in front of me. Still nothing.

Feeling silly, I lean down and check under the couch, hoping to see two sets of cat eyes staring back at me, but they aren't there. I know they haven't escaped out the front door and onto the street. They just don't want to see me.

I'm being snubbed by my own cats. Clearly, when it comes to pet parenting, I'm anything but a natural. But those two little sneaks are stuck with me now, so I guess we're all just going to need to figure out how to make this work.

I setup the new food and water dishes as quietly as I can, trying to appear calm and non-threatening, then move to do the same to the litterbox. Hopefully, neither cat has decided to use my laundry or some hidden corner as a makeshift bathroom in the meantime because if they did, I may never know about it.

By eight at night there's still no sign of the, and I've about reached my limit on how much playing it cool I'm capable of doing. I've spent the afternoon and evening moving slowly, talking in a low and hopefully soothing voice even though there's no reason for me to be talking to anyone at all. I've tried to be as non-threatening as possible but haven't seen so much as the tip of a tail as a reward.

Maybe they really did find a way to get out of here

without me knowing.

Even though I try to stay in one place on my couch, attempting to remain as still as I can, the idea won't loosen the hold it has on my mind.

If they have gotten out, the longer I wait the longer it will take to get them back. I don't even know if these cats have been outside before. Even so, I could see how they might trust the promise of the outdoors over that of the stranger who carried them to this place in cages.

Which leaves the question of where two cats might hide.

I start my hunt under the couch, which is still dust and clutter free only because I haven't lived here long, but the hunt only gets more ridiculous from there. I'm not sure how a cat might have gotten into the cupboard above my stove, but I check there anyway. And the space behind the toilet, and inside of the bathtub. But this at least is one benefit to living in such a small apartment. All that's left is the bedroom. And if I don't find them there, I can start wandering the neighborhood and freaking the fuck out.

I'm already trying to come up with a game plan for finding two cats who don't know me at all as I kneel down on the floor of my bedroom and find a set of green eyes blinking slowly at me from the farthest corner behind my bed. Walter lies curled around Simon watching me intently as the other cat sleeps, or pretends to. Well at least they're still here and getting along.

I go to bed that night hyper aware of the two tiny forms cuddled beneath me. I half expect them to bolt as soon as I lay down, but the three of us stay there together, all still and quiet, adjusting to our new way of life.

When I wake the next morning there's no sign of either of them but both the food and water bowls are lower than I remember, and someone has left me a present in the litterbox.

They're alive, so that counts for something.

I think about those cats all day at work as I slog through the endless pile of paperwork my boss left on my desk first thing Monday morning. My lunch is spent doing all of the research I probably should have done before I adopted two cats—what they need, and more importantly, how to win them over—and for the first time since I started my new job I catch the first bus back home after the end of the work day.

Walter is sitting on the couch when I get home, back straight as he tilts his head to look at me when I come in the door.

"Hi," I say quietly, cautiously and take another step into the room. He only blinks a response. I so badly want to approach him, and see if he'll let me rub his head the way he did in the shelter, but I don't push my luck. Instead I head for the kitchen to make myself a snack. When I get back to the living room, he's still there.

Moving slowly, I take my phone out of my back pocket and tap the screen to life before pulling up my camera. Walter is still looking particularly statuesque as I snap a few pictures zooming in rather than actually trying to get closer. But he's not looking at me anymore. He seems completely unconcerned that we are sharing a room.

Tess did say he was friendly, so maybe human interaction is something he'll be interested in. As long as I don't start yelling and waving my hands around in the air I probably won't hurt the already minimal trust he has in me.

I decide to risk it sitting down on the couch cushion beside the one my new cat had chosen to occupy. We're less than two feet apart and he still hasn't moved. He turns to look at me right when I shift my gaze over to him and we study each other for a long minute.

I lift my hand from my lap fully intending to reach over toward him and see how he reacts, but before my fingers are more than an inch off my jeans, I chicken out. I grab the remote control instead turning on the television and trying to force myself to go back to my usual after work routine. The sooner I start acting like myself the sooner these cats will figure out what it means to live here with me.

Or at least Walter will. There's still no sign of Simon.

An entire sitcom ticks by before Walter moves at all but soon his tiny body rests directly against my leg.

This is really happening! I let my fingers gently settle against the fur on Walter's back more than half expecting him to flee as soon as we touch, but he doesn't so much as flinch. Instead I could swear he pushes back up into my hand, just a little, welcoming the contact.

I think maybe I've made a friend. If I can manage to not screw this up.

Over the course of the next week, somehow, I don't. Walter never goes so far as to solicit my attention, but when I'm home he's always near by and that means everything to me. Even though I have to work a little bit harder to win Simon over I'm more than up to the challenge. It doesn't take me long to realize that the key to winning over my second cat is through his stomach. Whenever I fill up the food dishes I catch a glimpse of gray fur pacing outside the kitchen. As soon as I leave he's right there shoving his face into the bowl for a few seconds at a time.

He always looks up to make sure I know that he knows I'm watching him. Like he doesn't want me thinking I'm getting away with anything. But he lets me get close enough to snap a few pictures of him as well.

And after one full week living with cats I finally post pictures of my new babies up on Facebook to share with my friends and family from back home. Immediately, I'm bombarded with excitement and advice. I don't think I realized just how many people in my life consider themselves to be cat people. Without my even asking them to friends I haven't spoken to since high school start sending me pictures of their own cats, and I find myself appreciating their adorable furry faces more than I ever would have before.

My mom is the one who finally helps me win over Simon, encouraging me to feed him from my hand until he is more comfortable being around me.

After a month I have an Instagram account dedicated to Simon and Walter. Granted, I don't have a lot of followers, but it gives me a good excuse to take as many pictures as I want. Which even I can admit is a pretty ridiculous amount.

But they are so damn cute.

Unfortunately, not much else has changed for me. If anything I've been staying at home even more often since there are two other things living there who count on me. I buy groceries and cat food, take the bus everywhere, and I take pictures of my cats. But the routine is kind of nice.And I work. Five days a week, usually longer hours than are required, always reminding myself that this part of my life is a stepping stone on my way to bigger and better things.

Or something.

After another relaxing weekend lounging around my apartment, usually with one cat on my lap and the other somewhere behind me on the back of the couch, I return to work and an exceptionally cluttered desk. It's going to be a long week.I'm filing my fifteenth report of the day when I can't sit still a moment longer. My knees creak a little as I stand, protesting their lack of use.

I don't actually need anything other than a change of pace, so I head toward the main coffee machine on our floor of the office, and I'm actually a little relieved to find a near empty pot. I pour myself the last cup and then set about making the next batch, glad for the chance to avoid work a bit longer.

Sometimes it's hard to remember the version of myself who thought taking this job was going to be the most amazing experience of my life. At least now I can see that an opportunity and a genuinely enjoyable experience are not the same thing.

"Hey," a female voice says, coming up from behind me.

I mirror back a hello automatically before turning to see Jane-Anne, a data processor who I've seen in a few meetings. Her desk sits closest to the coffee station, and she always seems to be taking full advantage of the positioning, so I see her every few days. "It should just be a few minutes."

"No problem. I'm just killing time until lunch at this point anyway." Jane-Anne turns to lean the small of her back against the edge of the counter, turning to face the open space of our office. She pushes a lock of warm-brown hair out of her face before shifting her focus back to me.

I should say something. Anything. Something to break the ice and push our rapport past these brief conversations about caffeine. But as usual, I come up short.

Despite countless Google searches about how to make friends as an adult my tongue always ends up paralyzed whenever I have the chance to get to know people at work. Before moving to New Hapsburry I considered myself a pretty friendly person, but here, all I can manage is to imagine all of the ways I could embarrass myself in a town where I don't even have any friends to commiserate with.

I wait for the new pot to finish and top up my own glass, walking in awkward silence beside Jane-Anne, as we both head back to our work stations.

While she sets her own purple mug down on her desk I look over long enough to see a framed picture, sitting beside the coaster she's using. I must have seen that same frame every day since I first got up enough of a nerve to take coffee breaks at work, but for the first time I see the picture my new co-worker has placed there.

A picture of a yellow-eyed calico stares up at me.

"You have a cat?" I blurt out before I've passed her desk, not giving myself the chance to chicken out and keep my mouth shut.

Jane-Anne grins right away. "That's Sheela. I've had her since she was a kitten."

"She's gorgeous," I answer back. And she is. Maybe her patchy fur isn't something I would have appreciated a few months ago, but now her coat offers an undeniable common ground between me and someone who maybe doesn't have to be a stranger for much longer.

"I just adopted a couple of cats. They've basically taken over my life."

"Oh, I know! Sheela is the undeniable queen of my apartment."

Being owned by a cat seems to be a pretty universal experience. But the silence is already growing thicker around us, and I have to say something else quickly or give up and get back to work.

It's now or never.

"Hey," I say as Jane-Anne looks away to go back to her work. I can't remember the last time I was this nervous. "Did you have any plans for lunch?"

My co-worker's eyes find mine after the longest moment ever and I hold my breath as she starts to speak. I know this was probably the most casual request I could have made beyond asking to borrow a pen, but it still feels like I'll never be able to show my face in the office again if she says no.

"I was going to head across the street to grab that soup and sandwich combo deal that Forchelli's is advertising."

Oh.

"Did you want to come?"

Oh!

"Sure!" Did that sound too eager? Maybe. But I'm more than happy to live with sounding like a dork if it means I finally have some real plans.

"I'll see you later then?"

"Absolutely."

Kellie Bean is the contemporary fiction pen name of Kellie Sheridan. For more stories about finding your way (and usually finding lost pets) visit kelliesheridan.com

Love to read? Visit Patchwork-Press.com to find your next favorite series and your new favorite author!!

Other Patchwork Press Anthologies
The Lost Locket of Lahari
Polaris Awakening

www.ingramcontent.com/pod-product-compliance
Lightning Source LLC
Chambersburg PA
CBHW022145240626
47153CB00007B/2526